DEVERELL'S DILEMMA

DEVERELL'S DILEMMA

•

Kaye Calkins

AVALON BOOKS
NEW YORK

Published by Avalon Books,
an imprint of Thomas Bouregy & Co., Inc.
New York, NY

Library of Congress Cataloging-in-Publication Data

Calkins, Kaye.
    Deverell's dilemma / Kaye Calkins.
        p. cm.
    ISBN 978-0-8034-7462-8 (hardcover : alk. paper)
1. Young men—England—London—Fiction.   2. Rejection
(Psychology)—Fiction.   3. Murder—Investigation—
London—Fiction.   4. Triangles (Interpersonal relations)—
Fiction.   I. Title.
    PR6103.A44D48 2012
    823'.92—dc22

                                                        2011033918

PRINTED IN THE UNITED STATES OF AMERICA
ON ACID-FREE PAPER
BY RR DONNELLEY, HARRISONBURG, VIRGINIA

To my husband, Merle, and my critique group,
Barb, Diana, Jean, and Kathy,
for their input and unflagging support.
Also Pat Elliott for her encouragement and help.

Chapter One

1818

The brisk morning air fanned Deverell's face as he put the filly through her paces near his home outside of London. Spirited and a smooth gait, he thought. Father had chosen well, but would his scatterbrained brother appreciate this generous gift? Twenty years old, out of university, and Nat didn't have a modicum of common sense.

The thrashing of something in the undergrowth beside the lane grabbed his attention, and he reined in his mount. A large stallion burst from the yew hedge in front of him. The slender youth on its back pulled hard on the reins and called to the animal.

"Idiot," Deverell fumed under his breath. He quieted the filly with a pat on her neck. "Steady, girl." Her muscles quivered beneath his hand, and her breath hung in a mist on the cold air. Lucky for him she didn't spook easily.

He watched the bay career down the lane, the rider out of control. He gave Lady a light touch, urging her to close the gap between them and the bay. When they were side by side, Deverell reached out and grabbed the lad.

"Release the reins—I have you." Deverell's arm went around the boy's slender waist.

"No!" the youth yelled as he was lifted from his horse. "Let go of me."

Deverell reined in the mare with one hand and held on to the squirming figure perched on his horse in front of him.

"Sit still," he ordered. "You'll have us both on the ground."
Ungrateful imp.

"Let me down, you fool."

When Lady came to a full stop, Deverell relinquished his hold. The boy slid off in a heap onto the dirt moist from last night's rain.

Deverell's lips curved in a smile as he watched the boy shove his pant legs into his boots and pull his cap down around his ears.

"Of all the dim-witted, ramshackle things to do. Now I'll have to walk home." The rider looked up at Deverell, eyes flashing with anger.

"You're welcome. I make a habit of chasing down runaways whose riders can't restrain them." The sarcastic rejoinder slid from Deverell's tongue with ease.

"I was in perfect control. A hare startled the horse, and he bolted, but I wasn't in danger of falling off." A frown creased his brow.

Deverell chortled at the boy's bravado. "Come. I'll give you a ride." He held out his hand.

"Not on your life." The boy held his hands behind his back.

"Don't be stubborn. We may find your mount along the way." The child was stubborn to a fault. Deverell saw a flash of recognition in the challenging look from the sea-green eyes, but he'd never seen the lad before—must be someone's groom or stable hand. "What is your name?"

"Al . . . Alex."

"Let me give you a hand up, Alex."

Deverell grasped the small hand and hoisted the youth onto the back of his brother's horse. It was a soft hand for a groom. The faint scent of lavender floated on the air as Lady trotted forward.

A bend in the road revealed a large meadow with grasses bent heavy with moisture.

"There's your horse, feeding beside the lane. Now you won't

have to explain to your master why he came back without his rider."

Alex gave a muffled snort and slipped off the side of the mare. He whistled to the bay. The stallion pricked his ears and turned toward the sound. "Come, Prince."

The boy mounted the horse in one graceful move and set off through the meadow. Deverell watched them gallop across the field and leap a small stream. The lad's cap flew from his head and floated down as the gelding's hooves hit the ground.

Deverell broke into laughter. "I've been properly fooled." He gazed at the auburn hair that covered the shoulders and flowed out behind the rider as she sped away. A young woman dressed as a stable boy. She'd sounded like one too. What owner in his right mind would let her ride a horse like that bay? Must be an interesting story behind the masquerade.

Drat. Alexi stole a glance behind her. He was still in the lane. She urged her horse into a run. These early-morning rides were her favorite part of the day, and she wouldn't let a bumbling Sir Galahad spoil them.

She guided the horse behind the stables, slid off, and opened a side door. There were no voices inside, but she could hear Jem whistling in one of the stalls.

"Jem," she called. She slipped inside.

"Yes, miss, I'm comin'." The boy appeared around the corner, pitchfork in hand.

"Walk Prince and cool him down before you brush and feed him."

"I'll take good care of 'im, miss." He stabbed the fork into the ground and brushed his hands on his breeches.

The smell of straw and horse droppings permeated the air in the stable, but Alexi barely noticed. Her heart was still pounding from her near accident. Of all people, it had to be Deverell Bromfield. She had thought of him often, although she hadn't seen him in years. He hadn't changed much. He was still rescuing people. She lifted the latch to an empty stall and moved the blanket that hid her petticoats and frock. When she finished dressing, she reached for the latch, only to have it pulled from her grasp.

"Where have you been, young lady?"

She gasped, her heart in her throat.

The door opened wide, and her brother, Lucian, stepped inside.

She let her breath out in a whoosh. "Jackanapes, I thought you were Father."

A grin spread over his even features and turned up the corners of his full lips. "You've been riding Prince astride and without an attendant. If I had been Father, you would have been in a hobble."

"Jem told you," said Alexi. "I trusted him."

"Don't be angry with the boy; he told me instead of Father. I heard what you said to him when you came in. Sounds as if you were riding that stallion hard."

"I wouldn't have if Dev . . ." She hesitated. She could feel the heat of a flush on her cheeks.

"Go on." Lucian crossed his arms across his broad chest and looked at her through half-closed eyes.

"I saw Deverell Bromfield in the lane."

"Bromfield?"

"Prince bolted when a hare startled him and ran into the road. Deverell thought he was a runaway, and he 'rescued' me." She gave an unladylike snort.

"Hurt your pride, hmm? You used to watch Deverell with calf's eyes when you were younger."

She glared at Lucian. "He didn't even recognize me."

"You can be thankful for that." He plucked a piece of straw from her sleeve and another from her hair. "Your behavior was unbecoming a young lady. Those three years at Madame Pomphrey's Académie apparently did nothing for you." He shook a finger in her face.

"Of all the high-flown, arrogant . . ." She looked into his blue eyes, which were brimming with laughter.

He put his arm around her and gave her waist a squeeze. "I'm starved. Let's go in to breakfast."

"It's good to be home. I've missed you." She gave his cheek a sisterly peck.

"From now on, when you want to take an early-morning jaunt, I'll ride with you. You may wear any costume you please."

Her smile of delight faded when she remembered their father's remark that morning. "Lucian, I heard Papa say that you're gambling heavily at New Market. Is it true?"

"My life's not fodder for discussion." And suddenly his voice sounded sharp as steel.

A week later there was a knock on Deverell's office door. The clerk, Edgar, poked his head in and announced, "Fielding Stanhope to see you, sir."

"Send him in. Take these invoices and file them." He reached for a stack of papers on a corner of the desk and handed them to the young man.

Edgar held the door for Stanhope. The noise from the textile machinery drifted in with the stout young man.

"Glad to see you, Bromfield. It's been an age."

Deverell welcomed his friend with a handshake. "What brings you to town?"

"Family business. I saw Lucian Moreton an hour ago. He's renting rooms in town and wondered if we'd like to join him for dinner. I said yes on the outside chance you'd be free."

"I'll join you. I haven't seen Lucian in a while. Whatever possessed him to take rooms? The family has a home here in town as well as in Midfield."

"His father told him to finish his medical studies and join the family practice or enter the military."

Deverell raised his eyebrows. "And Lucian refused?"

"His grandfather left him a monthly allotment, so he moved to town. I've heard rumors he's been gaming and losing heavily."

"No doubt we'll find out more tonight." What had gotten into Lucian?

Stanhope put his hand on Deverell's shoulder. "No doubt, but I came to talk to you on a different matter. It's about your brother, Nathaniel."

With a heavy sigh Deverell asked, "What has the boy done now?" He removed a pile of papers from a chair and motioned Stanhope to sit.

The man sat down heavily and stretched his legs in front of him.

"Last week he came over to show me his new filly—a prime bit of horseflesh, by the way. My, uh, friend, Leticia was there with some others, and Nat spent the whole afternoon dangling after her. I wouldn't tell you, but this isn't the first time, and it's getting to be rather a bore. I finally sent him home."

Deverell leaned against the desk, his chin in his hand. "You can't be jealous. He's only a boy, and she is, shall we say, more sophisticated."

Stanhope's face flushed. "I just thought you ought to know. I'll set him down if I have to, but I'd rather not."

"He rarely listens to me, but I'll talk to him. Leticia is a flirt, and he's inexperienced with her kind. No offense meant."

"Just warn him off before I do." Stanhope stood and adjusted his top hat at an angle on his head.

Deverell saw his friend out of the office, then sat behind his desk drumming his fingers in a fast tattoo. Would the boy never learn to use common sense?

Chapter Two

Rising over the crest of the hillock, the sun colored the clouds pink and orange and set the crisp air glowing. Deverell inhaled the sweet scent of the swaying grasses beside the lane. Astride his favorite mount, he touched a heel to Queen Bess and felt the ripple of muscles as she moved into a canter. This morning's ride invigorated him as he followed the twisting path between stands of linden trees.

His life had settled into a pattern of work, riding, and church on Sunday. An occasional evening with friends comprised his social life. His brother said he was in a rut. Maybe he was, but he liked it. It was predictable. No heady intoxication of a love affair, and no anger and despair at the end of one. He was better off without a woman in his life.

The sound of thundering hooves reached him just before the horse and rider rounded the bend. *Not again,* he thought, as he pulled the filly into the trees to escape being run down. His topper, knocked from his head by a low-hanging limb, fell into the lane just as the bay galloped by.

Alexi saw the hat as it rolled onto the path. Too late. Prince was going to trample it. She glimpsed Deverell's scowling face as she flew past. Her lips drew up in a smirk that became a laugh as she headed across the field for home.

She felt the ground shake as a horse pulled up beside her. A hand grabbed and held her arm until she pulled the bay to a stop. She reached for the pommel and held on to control her shaking hands. Her hair fell loose from under her cap.

"How dare you?" she protested. "I could have fallen." *Too bad the limb hadn't knocked his head off.*

"Then I would have saved you again." He held on to her reins, and his filly danced around until they were face-to-face. "I'd like to know, young lady, what this masquerade is about and why you seem bent on running me down."

Alexi felt her face flush. She pulled the reins from his hand and kneed her horse into a run. The nerve of the man. To think she had once idolized him. She would make sure she didn't run into him again. She started to giggle. At least, not literally.

Deverell, intent on his work, didn't raise his head as Edgar set a large box on the desk.

"This came for you by messenger, sir."

"Thank you." Deverell glanced up. "But I didn't order anything. There must be some mistake."

Edgar pointed to the address. "Your name is on the top, sir."

Deverell opened the package and smiled as he drew a fine top hat from it. "It's a beauty. How did she know where to send it?"

"Will there be an answer, sir?" Curiosity written on his face, Edgar tried to conceal a grin.

Deverell searched the box for a note. "Hmm, no, no answer." He replaced the hat in the box and set it in a corner of the room. His gaze strayed to it often, provoking a slight smile. Who was this red-haired minx? Did he know her? It was kind of her to replace his topper. She couldn't be the daughter of a groom if she shopped at the most famous hatmaker in London.

"This is not a proper neighborhood for a lady to visit," said Abby.

"Don't be stuffy. If Lucian lives here, it must be respectable," said Alexi. "Honestly, sometimes ladies' maids can be so stodgy."

"Humph. And what kind of trouble will I be in if something happens to you?"

"Don't worry, Abby, we'll be perfectly safe. The driver is stopping; this must be the place."

Two men leaned against the stained rock wall of the terraced house. Rusted iron handrails lined three brick steps that led to a faded green door.

"Pay the man, Abby," said Alexandra as she alighted from the cab. She glanced at the men, who gave her a bold stare. She lifted her chin slightly, climbed the steps, and knocked loudly with the tarnished brass knocker. "Be careful of the second stair; one of the bricks is loose," she warned her companion.

Both women waited on the small porch. "Whoever answers the door is taking her own sweet time," said Abby.

"That would be the owner, Mistress Dinwiddie," said the younger of the two men, his gaze assessing the women.

Abby sniffed and turned her back on him. Alexandra knocked again.

The door opened, and a middle-aged woman whose plump figure was still curvaceous peeked out. "I don't take in women boarders. Sorry, ladies." She started to shut the door.

"I am here to visit Lucian Moreton." Alexandra pushed it open.

"I don't allow no women in the men's quarters neither. Besides, 'e don't come down 'til noon."

"I am his sister, and this is my Abigail." She stepped inside, followed by Abby. "Now, will you please tell my brother I am here?"

"'Is rooms are on the third floor. 'Elp yerself." The woman turned and walked into the sitting room.

The narrow stairs, though worn with usage, were clean and polished, as was the hall leading to Lucian's rooms. A narrow window lit the way. Alexandra knocked. Hearing a groan, she knocked louder. At last Lucian opened the door wide enough to peer out.

"Alexi, what are you doing here? How did you get past old Dinwiddie?"

"I told her I was your sister. Let us in, please." She pushed the door farther open.

" 'Us'?" He pulled his dressing gown tighter around him and pushed his hair out of his eyes. "Oh. It's you, Abby."

"Good morning, sir," she said with a sniff.

"You look queer as Dick's hatband, Lucian. Are you getting enough sleep? I've brought the money for that purchase you made for me," said Alexi.

"Thanks. Lay it on the table while I dress." He closed the door to the bedroom.

Alexi noticed that the sitting room was clean but shabby. A small square table and two straight-back chairs took up one corner. A sofa stood against a wall, a worn carpet in front. Leaded glass windows framed the undersized fireplace across the room. She wished Lucian wasn't so stubborn. If only he'd do what Father wanted.

"Sit down, Abby. It may be a while."

Half an hour passed before the bedroom door opened. "Would you ladies like to join me for a walk to the bakery down the street? I am starved."

Dressed in a morning coat and trousers, he looked quite handsome. Alexi took her brother's arm and asked him, "Are you quite well, Lucian?"

He patted her arm. "I'm fine, but it's nice to know you care. To tell the truth, I've been hobnobbing with nobility. Have you heard of Lord Brendan Helmsley? He is introducing me around. Last night I went to a salon hosted by the widow of Viscount Chatham."

"My goodness, aren't we stepping up in the world," was all Alexandra could say. Her heart was heavy with trepidation for him.

Alexi and her mother were embroidering pillowcases in the morning room when the maid entered. "Mrs. Bromfield to see you, ma'am."

"Show her in, please, and bring us a fresh pot of tea," said Isabel Moreton. She put her sewing in the large basket beside her and straightened the skirt of her blue flower-sprigged muslin.

"You didn't tell me you were having visitors this morning, Mother. I'll take my embroidery upstairs." Alexi rose and turned toward the door.

"Mrs. Bromfield will be delighted to see you, Alexi. Stay and have a cup of tea with us."

"All right." If Deverell had told his mother about the runaway horse, she would be mortified.

The door opened, and a smiling woman entered. Her yellow dress and brown pelisse set off her dark brown eyes and hair.

"Anne Louise, come in. So good to see you." Mrs. Moreton rose and hastened across the room to give her friend a hug. "You remember Alexandra?" She motioned her daughter forward.

"Yes, how nice to see you. You have been away at school, I believe."

"I'm finished now and glad to be home," replied Alexi, who had risen at the older woman's entrance.

"Please sit down over here by the fire. I have ordered tea," Isabel said. After a soft knock on the door, the parlor maid brought in a tray and placed it in front of her.

"Thank you," said Mrs. Bromfield, as she accepted a cup of tea. "Have you seen the Eddingtons lately? Weren't you and Penelope chums, Alexandra?"

"Yes, we are. I haven't seen her since I came home, but I am sure I shall. That reminds me. Mother, my friend Caroline Witherspoon invited me to visit her in London this month."

"That's nice, dear. Have one of these biscuits, Anne Louise; they are one of Cook's best."

As Isabel passed the plate to her friend, she asked Alexandra, "Is your friend's mother Delia Witherspoon, the woman with a multitude of ailments?"

"The very same, Mother. Don't tell me she is seeing Father."

"When I was in town last week, I met her in his office. She has been seeing him every week for two months. Oh, dear, I should not have repeated that."

"Everyone knows what she is like. She goes on about her illnesses ad nauseum. Caroline takes care of her without a word of reproach. She is hardly ever free to be with people her own age." Alexi set down her cup. "I must take my leave now. I have some chores to do. It has been nice to see you again, Mrs. Bromfield."

Alexi kissed her mother's cheek and took her sewing upstairs.

"Your daughter has grown into a beautiful young woman, Isabel. Her auburn hair, even tucked under her cap, is a crowning glory."

Isabel smiled. "We sent her to Madame Pomphrey's Académie. I had given up hope of keeping her out of trees and riding her pony bareback. I am thankful she has become a charming young woman. Oh, dear, I hope I don't sound boastful."

Anne Louise laughed. "You sound like a mother. As for my own sons, Nathaniel sometimes worries me, but he'll grow up soon, I hope. Deverell, on the other hand, is a great help to his father in the textile mill. I do wish he would show more interest in finding a wife, though. I can't help thinking the disastrous affair with that young woman a couple of years ago has soured him on the whole gender."

"Oh, surely not."

"As far as his father and I know, he has shown no interest in any woman since."

"Did you know that Alexandra had a tendre for Deverell when she was a child? She followed all three of the boys, but she stuck to Deverell like a burr. Lucian was always complaining to me, but Deverell never seemed to mind. He even rescued her when her pony ran away."

"Hmm, are you thinking what I am thinking?" asked Anne Louise.

"Deverell and Alexandra?" A smile lit Isabel's eyes.

"Why not? They just might suit."

"How do we get them together?" Isabel moved closer to her friend and took her hand.

"If we put our heads together, I am sure we will come up with something."

* * *

Friday night, when her husband, Fredrick, arrived from London, Anne Louise had his favorite savory meat pie with her special herbed crust ready for his dinner. Cook was baking his favorite custard.

The aroma filled the house as his wife met him at the door.

"Do I detect a meat pie in the oven, Mrs. Bromfield?" He put his arm around her and gave her a squeeze.

"You are very perceptive, Mr. Bromfield. First you shall have a warm bath to rid yourself of the smell of the city and your horse."

He kissed her cheek. "You spoil me, dear lady." His voice was warm.

Later that evening they made ready for bed. She braided her hair at the dressing table, and he read by the gas lamp above the bed.

"Fredrick?"

"Hmm?"

"I would like to have a dinner party this month, a few guests. What do you think?"

He chuckled. "I wondered when you would get around to your request. My favorite dinner and dessert, and you wore the blue dress I like. I knew there was something."

She turned to him with a smile. "Fredrick, even Queen Esther dressed in her finest and served a banquet before she asked a favor of the king."

"Come here and sit beside me." He patted the bed. "I was only teasing. You'll have your dinner party. Who are you planning to invite?"

"The Moretons and Alexandra, the Eddingtons and their two daughters, and Fielding Stanhope and his mother, Esmerelda." She ticked them off on her fingers.

"An interesting group. Esmerelda is as flighty as ever, I suppose. Stanhope would have become a better man if he'd had a father's steady influence."

"He's done well with the business and land holdings his father left him. Deverell doesn't say much, but I gather Fielding's social life is not what it should be."

"Gambling, drinking, and women, I hear," said her husband. "I am sorry for the young man but thankful he is not our problem."

I pray Nat does not follow that path, thought his mother. She turned off the gas lamp and slid into bed. A frown wrinkled her brow, and a tiny sigh escaped her lips.

Chapter Three

A dinner party at the Bromfields'? I won't be able to make it," said Alexandra. "That is the week I am invited to Caroline's in London." She couldn't face Deverell.

"You'll have to beg off from Caroline's, I'm afraid. I have already accepted the Bromfields' invitation for all of us."

"But, Mother, you didn't ask me." Her voice was a whine even to her own ears.

"I thought you would be eager to attend and see some of your old friends again. The Eddington girls, Penelope and—what's the younger girl's name?"

"Chloe. She is hardly out of the schoolroom."

"Mrs. Moreton has invited an even number of young people. We cannot upset her table arrangement, and if there is dancing, there must be the same number of young guests."

"Dancing? You know I hate dancing."

"That's enough. We are all going to the dinner party in three weeks. We must have dresses made. Soft rose for me and a nice green for you, if you'd like."

No use arguing with her mother. Alexi could see that her mind was made up. "Green will be fine. Something sophisticated." Maybe he wouldn't recognize her.

"I am surprised you're not eager to see Deverell. He was a favorite of yours when you were younger."

"Mama, I was only fifteen."

"And now you are an old lady of nineteen. My, how time flies. You haven't seen him in several years. You may still find him attractive."

"It wasn't his looks I admired; it was his kindness. He was patient with me and didn't get angry like Lucian. I am sure his personality has altered."

"How can you possibly know that?"

"People change, Mama." *You didn't see his brown eyes flash with anger.* "I'll write and see if I can visit Caroline earlier. I'll look for a bonnet to go with my new dress while I'm in London. Do you think the dressmaker could make a snood to match the green dress?"

"I hear they are all the rage," said her mother. She touched one of Alexandra's curls. "Although it's a shame to cover your beautiful hair."

That was precisely what she wanted, something to cover her hair. "I think I shall see what flowers are blooming. I'll bring some in for the dining room." What had possessed the Bromfields to have a dinner party now, of all times? Christmas would have been a much better time. It was months away.

Alexi tied the blue ribbons of the straw hat under her chin. The gardening smock hung on a hook beside the door. She slipped it over her head and took the old gloves from the pocket. Picking up a basket and sliding it over her arm, she pushed open the kitchen door. The gravel crunched beneath her slippers as she stepped outside. The sharp fragrance of rosemary and sage filled the air. Through the picket gate and under the arbor of vines, whose leaves were beginning to unfurl, she walked to her mother's rose garden. Deep-colored leaves covered the stalks, but it was too early for blooms. Beyond that the spring flowers were a riot of color: pink cranesbill, red campion, and marigolds. She bent to examine the white hogweed. Such an ugly name for such a pretty flower, she thought.

She noticed the purple aubretia was overtaking one of the flower beds. She put on the gloves, knelt, and took her trowel to dig out some of the plants. A dinner party at the Bromfields' and dancing. What should she do? She swiped a finger across her face to pull back a lock of hair and left a smear of dirt across her cheek. Engrossed in her work, she did not hear the footsteps on the gravel behind her.

"Good day. I have come to bring . . . I am sorry. I thought you were Mrs. Moreton."

The deep male voice reached her ears before she raised her gaze to expressive eyebrows drawn together in a puzzled frown. She gazed into dark brown eyes flecked with gold highlights. His lips were full and drawn up into a quizzical smile. The jaw was squared and set off by a dimple in the chin.

"I . . . I am sorry, sir." Her mouth was dry.

"Is your mistress in?"

She cleared her throat. "I'll see, sir."

She jumped up and stumbled over the basket that lay behind her. Deverell reached out and firmly gripped her arms to keep her from falling. He looked into her eyes, and Alexi dropped her lashes. She stepped back, and Deverell released her.

"Are you all right?" he asked.

"I . . . I'm fine, sir." She ducked her head.

"Have you worked here long?"

"Not long, sir." Her voice was low and deferential.

"Hmm." His forehead puckered in a frown.

"I'll go tell the mistress there is someone to see her."

"Thank you. I shall present myself at the front door."

Alexi looked back as she entered the kitchen door and smiled at the bemused look on his face.

She called to the cook. "Send the parlor maid to answer the door. There is a gentleman on his way."

She waited by the kitchen door until she was sure he had gone around the corner. The grove of apple trees would make a good place to wait until he left the property. She promptly raced there and climbed into a sheltering tree. Her mother might expect her to help entertain their guest, but she could not face him. And how could she have forgotten those gold-flecked eyes? Her heart had somersaulted when she gazed into them. The firm jaw and the dimple in the chin were very appealing too, when the rest of the face wasn't angry.

Arms around her knees and her skirts tucked under her, she nestled in the crotch of the tree. Apple blossoms covered Alexi like a thick white cloud. It was not long until she heard the clipped sound of horse's hooves as Deverell passed down the lane and continued into the road. She held her skirts and jumped from the tree, then dashed to the garden, where she retrieved the basket of flowers and her tools. The kitchen door slammed shut as she headed for the back stairs and her room.

There was a tap on Alexi's bedroom door, and her mother entered. "Where have you been, girl? We had a visitor. I thought you might help me entertain him. I must say that Deverell Bromfield has matured into a handsome and mannerly gentleman."

"Deverell? Why would he be visiting here?" She was sitting by the window with a book in her lap.

"He brought me a message from Lucian. I find it quite refreshing that a busy young man would find the time to bring a message to his friend's mother."

"How is Lucian?"

"He said he was well and sent his love." She pulled two white petals out of Alexi's hair. "What were you doing? You have dirt smudged across your cheek, and I believe these are apple blossoms."

"I went into the grove to smell the blooms."

Her mother gave a slight frown. "Deverell told me he talked to one of the servant girls in the garden. Didn't you say you were going to pick a bouquet? Are you trying to avoid Deverell Bromfield?"

"Now, Mama, why would I do that?" She felt her cheeks flush.

"I don't know, but I'm sure there's a story there, somewhere." Her mother gave her a sideways glance and pursed her lips.

Alexi picked up the hand mirror from the bureau. *Oh, dear.* That smudge had been there when she talked to Deverell. She dipped a cloth into the bowl of water and scrubbed. No wonder he'd thought she was a servant.

Chapter Four

Deverell sighed as he leaned his forearm against the window of the drawing room. No escape now. Two carriages stood at the door, and a brougham rolled up the drive beside a lone rider. He should have stayed in London.

Nat rushed into the room, the ends of his cravat streaming behind him. "Sorry I'm late, Mother, Father. Help me, Dev. I can't tie this."

Deverell took the ends of the cravat and bent down to make a Gordian knot. "There, little brother, it's done."

"You'd think, now that I am twenty, you could stop calling me 'little' brother," the younger man complained.

"When you no longer ask me to rescue you from your scrapes, I will," Deverell said.

Nat grinned sheepishly and took a seat by his mother.

Deverell stood facing the fireplace, his eyes on the mantel clock. Another boring dinner party. It wasn't that he disliked his parents' friends and their children, although except for Stanhope, the young people attending were just out of the schoolroom. He didn't enjoy small talk, nor the simpering compliments that went with it. Why had he let his mother talk him into it?

"Your guests have arrived, ma'am," Williams, the butler, informed Mrs. Bromfield.

"We will be there directly," she replied.

Mr. Bromfield took her arm and led the family to the foyer, where they formed a line to receive their guests. A great deal of conversation and laughter preceded the crowd as they spilled into the entrance hall. The ladies' dresses added splashes of blue, rose, and yellow to the room, reflected by the large wall mirrors. The Eddingtons approached first.

Deverell bowed to the two young women. *What were their names? Ah, yes.* "Miss Penelope and Miss Chloe, how delightful to see you again." *That* was a simpering compliment if ever he'd heard one.

"How kind of you to remember," said the elder, Penelope.

His mother greeted Mrs. Stanhope. "We are glad you could come. You are looking well."

Esmerelda Stanhope patted her hand. "Anne Louise, so nice of you to invite my son and me."

Deverell gave Fielding Stanhope a rueful smile and grasped his hand. "Glad you are here, old friend. At least I shall have someone to talk to."

Stanhope raised his eyebrows. "Perhaps I should have brought Leticia."

"Certainly not." Deverell gave him a stern look.

Stanhope's grin was wide in his rather ordinary face. "I'll try not to mortify your parents; I'll be on my best behavior this evening. Have you heard the latest *on dits* from London? I'll regale you with them later."

Shaking his head slightly, Deverell watched Fielding walk away. Stanhope knew he didn't care about the latest gossip. Deverell rubbed his chin. He had to admit the man was always in the height of fashion. His tailor knew how to cut his coats in spite of his stocky build.

His father welcomed Dr. Moreton and bowed to his wife. "I understand you are to be congratulated, sir."

"Yes, I was surprised when I got the letter informing me of the honor. I never expected a knighthood. I was just practicing my profession."

"I suppose we shall have to call you Sir Rowland now," Fredrick said, chuckling.

"Our friendship is too old to stand on ceremony, Bromfield." He clasped the other man's shoulder.

"Glad to hear it." His father chuckled again.

"Nice to see you again, Mrs. Moreton," Deverell said as he bowed over her hand.

"Deverell, it has been far too long. I remember when you, Fielding, and my Lucian spent a lot of time at our home. Alas, those days are gone." Her mouth sagged, and Deverell thought he saw a tear in her eye. She crossed the room and took Mrs. Eddington's arm. *Why the tear? Over Lucian maybe?* He leaned over to speak to his mother, when a slender young woman in a pale green silk dress appeared before him. She held out her hand, and he brought it to his lips.

"Good evening, Dev . . . Mr. Bromfield. You don't recognize me, do you?"

Her laugh delighted his ears and prodded his memory. There was something familiar about this auburn-haired beauty.

"Alexi?" he gasped. The skinny tomboy had grown up. What had happened to the mop of hair that flew in every direction, the torn stockings and dirty smocks?

"Miss Alexandra Moreton, if you please." Her sea-green eyes sparkled. "You did not recognize me. Admit it."

He found it hard to take his gaze from her face. "Forgive me, but it has been several years, and you are hardly the gangly child I knew." He continued to hold her hand.

"It has been four years, and you have not changed a bit. Deverell the gallant, with a pretty compliment on your lips."

"I did not mean that." He look chagrinned.

"Of course you did. I *was* rather gangly, and my curly hair was always flying in my face. I remember you used to tease me about it."

He took her by the arm and led her to a corner of the drawing room. "Tell me, where have you been?"

She smoothed her skirt as she sat down. "I was away at Madame Pomphrey's Académie for Young Ladies for three years. My mother thought I needed to stop climbing trees and change my hoydenish ways."

Deverell gave a low chuckle. "I'm sure it was terribly boring."

He couldn't imagine her confined to a schoolroom learning French and playing the piano.

"Dreadfully, but I must have changed, for you did not recognize me, sir."

"No, I must admit, you do not look much like the little girl who followed her brother and his friends everywhere. I understand Lucian is living in London."

Her brow puckered in a frown, and he had an urge to smooth it out with the tip of his finger.

Williams announced dinner, and Deverell took Alexandra's arm to lead her to the dining room. The soft glow of the crystal chandeliers played over the planes and curves of her face. Deverell glanced down and let his breath out slowly. Her beauty sent heat waves through him; he hoped his face had not flushed. It had been a long time since a woman made him feel so disconcerted yet so exhilarated.

Deverell helped Alexandra with her chair and sat beside her. He glanced out of the corner of his eye to find her watching him.

He raised an eyebrow. "A penny for your thoughts."

"Maybe later. I understand you are working with your father. Does it suit you?" she asked.

He turned in his chair toward her. "The textile business is interesting. I enjoy it."

Why hadn't his mother told him Alexandra was such a beauty? Not that he'd shown interest in a woman for years.

"Do you still ride?" Deverell asked.

"Yes, I do." Alexandra arched her eyebrow. "Quite well now, actually."

"I did not mean to remind you of that embarrassing moment."

Her face turned a becoming shade of pink. "What moment are you speaking of?"

He flicked his fingers. "It's of no consequence. I believe there was a runaway."

Her eyes narrowed, and she turned away to speak to her mother.

Now what did I say? wondered Deverell.

After the fish was served, Deverell asked, "Do you still have that pony?"

"What pony is that?"

"The one that ran away with you."

"You mean Clover?" She gave a little laugh. "We still have her, although she is getting quite old."

"She was cantankerous. Bit me that day I rescued you." He still had a faint scar on his arm from it.

"Did she?"

He saw her lips twitch and her eyes glimmer before she looked down at her plate.

"I saw Lucian in London," he said.

Alexandra glanced down the table at her mother, then lowered her voice. "Mama told me you stopped by with a message from him. Could I ask you something about him later, please?"

"Of course." What had Lucian done to upset his mother and sister?

Alexandra was quiet during the rest of dinner, although Deverell did his best to draw her out.

After the dessert of egg custard and berries, the ladies withdrew to the drawing room to have tea while they awaited the men. The older women sat near the fireplace. The younger ones drew straight-backed chairs into a corner.

"He's very handsome," said Penelope, leaning close to the other two.

"Whom are you speaking of?" Alexandra asked.

"Mr. Bromfield, of course." She lifted the teacup to her lips.

"Yes, a very handsome older gentleman," Alexandra agreed, making a graceful gesture with her hand.

Penelope choked on her tea. " 'Older'? I meant young Mr. Bromfield."

Alexandra chuckled. "Deverell? I suppose you could call him handsome." Brown hair that waved back from his forehead and dark brown eyes with golden lights in them, well-shaped legs and broad shoulders. *Stop it, Alexi. You are supposed to dislike the man.*

Kaye Calkins

"You must have noticed, Alexandra," Penelope insisted. Her teacup rested on a small table beside her.

"Yes, you have been talking to him all evening," Chloe added with a smirk.

"I have known him since I was a child."

Mrs. Bromfield called to the girls. "Mrs. Eddington will play the piano if you girls would like to dance when the men join us."

Chloe clapped her hands.

"That'll be entertaining," said Penelope.

Alexandra grimaced. *Oh, no.* Even her dancing teacher at the académie had given up when she couldn't stay off her partner's toes.

Mrs. Bromfield called the servants in to rearrange the furniture, and the two sisters suggested some country dances. "The piano should be over there," Anne Louise Bromfield said to the butler. "What do you think, Sophorina?"

"Yes, that will be fine. It will be out of the way of the dancers," replied Mrs. Eddington.

Alexandra stayed in her chair, wishing she could disappear into the floor. She would make a fool of herself in front of Deverell, and he would see her as that gangly girl again. Still, why should she care what he thought? He was insufferable.

"There, everything is in place. The men will be in soon; won't they be surprised?" Mrs. Bromfield said.

Oh, they'll be surprised all right, thought Alexandra.

Deverell looked down the table through the haze of cigar smoke. Nat's elbow was on the table, his head resting on his palm.

"When will Father allow us to return to the ladies?" he mouthed to Deverell, then hid a yawn behind his hand.

"Well, gentlemen, let us return to the drawing room and join the ladies," said Mr. Bromfield, as if on cue.

The young men surged to the door as the older ones rose from the table. Deverell's gaze searched the room for Alexandra.

Mr. Bromfield said, "I see the ladies have been busy. It seems we are to have some entertainment. What have you planned, my dear?"

"Mrs. Eddington has agreed to play some reels and country dances." She pointed to the piano pushed back against a wall.

Stanhope headed toward Alexandra, only to find Deverell beside her.

"Sorry, old chap." Deverell grinned and raised one eyebrow.

"Then I shall ask for the second dance of the evening, Miss Moreton."

"As you wish, Mr. Stanhope."

"Gentlemen, I intend to have the first dance with my daughter." Mr. Moreton took her hand.

"Thank you, Papa," Alexi whispered as they took their place in the line.

"I saw you tapping your foot and thought I would rescue you."

"Oh, my, was it that noticeable?" She frowned.

"Only to your father, my dear." He patted her hand.

"I am not very agile on the dance floor."

"I am sure no one will notice," he encouraged her.

"Not until I step on his toes," she said, and her eyes twinkled.

The father and daughter joined the line of dancers.

Deverell bowed to Mrs. Moreton and led her onto the dance floor. He contrived to speak to Alexandra as they passed each other in the line dance. "We still must talk about Lucian."

"Fielding's dance is next," she said as she moved on to another partner.

Alexandra held her breath as Stanhope approached her and offered his arm. If she made it through this, she would sit out the rest of the evening.

"Lucian forgot to tell me his younger sister had become a beauty," Stanhope said, breathless from the energetic dance.

"You are such a tease, Mr. Stanhope. You must be careful, or someone may believe you." Alexandra passed on to the next partner, missing his toes by a fraction of an inch.

When the music ended, she said, "Take me back to my chair, please, and if you would be so kind, bring me some punch." She sighed with relief and rested on the chaise in a corner.

Stanhope made his way to the refreshment table by the door of the drawing room.

Deverell took the chair by Alexandra and handed her a cup.

"Thank you," she said. "You have saved my life again."

"You looked apprehensive, and your face was flushed." One side of his mouth lifted in a lopsided grin.

"I didn't want to step on my partners' toes."

"You don't like to dance?"

"I'd much rather climb trees or ride my horse." She held her breath. *Don't talk about horses,* she warned herself.

His low chuckle was warm and infectious. "Alexi, mischievous as ever."

"Harrumph." Stanhope had returned with her drink. "Beaten again," he said as he looked at the cup in her hand. "Ah, well, I am sure there is another thirsty young lady here. I see Penelope across the room. By the way, Deverell, I will be in London next week visiting a friend." He gave Deverell a sly wink over Alexandra's head. "Maybe we can have dinner one night."

"Let me know when, and I shall be glad to join you."

Deverell turned back to Alexi, his face serious. "What did you want to ask me about Lucian?"

She set the cup on the table beside her and was quiet for a moment. Her fingers pleated the material of her skirt. "Two months ago Papa paid off Lucian's gambling debts and gave him an ultimatum: start his training to become a doctor, or join the military. He had often said he would like to join Papa's practice. We were sure he would settle down and go back to school." She sighed and shook her head. "But the day his monthly allowance from Grandfather's trust started, he moved out. Mama is brokenhearted, and so is Papa. We have heard rumors that he is gambling heavily and has taken up with a woman. Papa is afraid he'll be leg-shackled to someone unsuitable."

Deverell's eyes widened.

"Do not give me that look, Deverell Bromfield. I learned those words from you and my brother when I was a child."

She could see the twinkle in his eyes when he asked, "How may I help?"

"You are his friend. Talk to him."

"I shall try, but I doubt if I can make him see reason. He must see it for himself."

She leaned forward in her chair and put her hand out toward him. "I know, but I am desperate to help my family."

He clasped her hand in both of his. "I will do what I can." Brown eyes with golden highlights held hers.

Alexi's cheeks grew warm. She hoped he couldn't read her thoughts.

Chapter Five

Deverell held the pen over the receipt book before him and gazed into space. *Alexi.* She was the reason he couldn't concentrate. A few years ago she was a child running after her brother, curly hair flying and smock dirty from climbing some tree or playing in the stables with the kittens. She was a woman now, with sea-green eyes he could swim in and wavy hair he wanted to run his fingers through. *Confound it!* He needed to be working. Where were those figures he was supposed to have for Father this morning? He drew the inkwell closer and selected a clean sheet of paper. First he would send a note to Lucian and fulfill his promise to Alexi.

That evening at the University Club, Deverell smiled at the young man whose blond hair was brushed forward in curls over his forehead. His eyes were hazel, more brown than green, unlike Alexi's.

"It was good of you to have dinner with me on such short notice, Lucian."

The two shook hands and sat down at a small table. Deverell leaned back in his chair.

"You are looking well, Deverell. Life must agree with you." Lucian twisted the ring on his little finger, and his gaze didn't meet Deverell's.

"I am sorry to say it, but you look as if you've been playing too hard. Been out all night?" asked Deverell.

"Good old Dev, never one to mince words." He gave a hollow laugh.

"We have been friends too long for that."

Lucian's back stiffened. "I have been out on the town, but it doesn't need to concern you. Everything is fine."

"Still gambling?"

"Who have you been talking to?" His anger was apparent in the set of his mouth and the glint in his eyes.

Deverell leaned forward and touched his friend's arm. "Don't get your bristles up. You look tired, and I wondered why."

"It's nothing." Lucian signaled for the waiter.

After they had placed their dinner order, Deverell said, "I understand your father was knighted for his medical work."

"He treated a member of the royal family, who recovered. I suppose that was considered worthy of a knighthood." Lucian folded and unfolded his napkin.

"You don't think so?"

He leaned forward across the table. "Deverell, I haven't seen my family in weeks. Father thinks I should become a doctor. I don't." He frowned, his eyes dark.

"When we were boys, I remember you wanted to be a doctor."

"Childish dreams, Bromfield." He shrugged his shoulders, then leaned back in his chair. "You wanted to go into the Army."

Deverell chuckled. "I see what you mean. Speaking of our childhood, remember the puppy Alexi brought to you with a hurt paw? You bandaged it, and she carried it around in a basket the rest of the afternoon." He remembered her green eyes swimming in tears when she brought Lucian the injured dog.

Lucian's eyes softened as he looked at Deverell. "We had some good times, you and I and Nat and Stanhope, with Alexi tagging along. What happened? Life has become so . . ."

What was that in his eyes? Pain? Loneliness? Dev wished he could help his friend.

Their conversation paused when the waiter arrived with their dinner. Lucian picked up his utensils and began to eat.

"Have you seen Stanhope since we had dinner together?" Deverell asked.

"Just the other day, as a matter of fact, here at the University Club. I think he was in town to see Leticia."

"Stanhope's latest light-o-love. He is much too free with these women. They take advantage of him."

"You sound like your father, Bromfield." Lucian picked up his glass.

Deverell smiled. "I suppose I do. So, have you found a fair lady to woo?"

Lucian gave a slight gasp and choked on the wine.

"Sorry, I did not mean to upset you. Are you all right?" Deverell started to rise.

Lucian waved his hand in answer and continued to cough. "I'm . . . fine."

"I take it that was a yes," said Deverell as he eased back into his chair.

"No, that is . . . no. There is no one."

Was Lucian's face red from choking, or was there another reason? An affair with some ladylove? Why wouldn't he say so?

Lucian had little more to say after that and soon took his leave.

Deverell hailed a hackney. He frowned as he climbed in. He had gained little information. What would he tell Alexi?

Her name evoked a curious sensation where his heart was supposed to be. He had been successful at ignoring any stirrings of attraction to a woman for so long, he'd thought he was immune. Could he open his heart again after Ariadne?

At their town home the butler met him at the door. "Your father is waiting for you in the study."

"Thank you, Chess." He turned down the hall and opened the door to the study.

Mr. Bromfield looked up as Deverell entered. "Did you have a nice dinner?"

"Yes, Father. I understand you wanted to see me."

"I looked over the figures you gave me. We are showing a nice, steady profit. I appreciate the job you are doing, son." Mr. Bromfield leaned back in his chair, clasped his hands over his stomach, and looked at Deverell. "Sit down. I'd like to talk to you. I know it is none of my business, but I noticed the other night that you were quite taken with Alexandra Moreton. I must say, she has grown into a beauty. Was I mistaken?" his father asked.

Deverell felt his palms grow sweaty. He had spent most of the dinner party with her, and he had enjoyed every moment of it. She was genuine and funny. His breath caught at the thought of her blush when he took her hands.

"I was certainly surprised by how she had changed. She's no longer the child I knew," Deverell answered.

"Pardon an old man's curiosity. It's just that your mother was wondering, and I thought I would ask. The Moretons are some of our oldest friends, and we can see no impediment to such an attachment, if you should pursue it."

"Thank you, Father. If that is all, I'll retire."

"Good night, son." Mr. Bromfield looked pleased as he rose and walked Deverell to the door.

"Good night, Father." Deverell strode toward the stairs, then took them two at a time. Sweat beaded on his forehead. His father's speech had set his heart racing with the memory of another time in that study three years ago.

He yanked the door to his bedroom open and almost ran into the butler. "I'm sorry, Chess." Deverell stepped out of the man's way.

"It's all right, sir. I have turned down your bed and laid out your night things. Will that be all?" At Deverell's nod, he shut the door.

Deverell sat down at his desk. He picked up the pen and made sure the inkwell was filled, then paused.

What was the matter with him? A few minutes ago he was eager to write to Alexi. He looked forward to seeing her again. Now . . .

He leaned forward, hands clasped on the desk. The image of a blue-eyed woman captured his mind. Blond hair, soft and shimmery like gold, skin like alabaster, feminine curves that

made men desire her, and a heart overflowing with love . . .
for herself. That was Ariadne. He had given her his heart,
asked her to marry him, and she had accepted.

He could still hear her warm voice. "Deverell, I had hoped,
dreamed, of the day you would ask. Of course I shall marry
you." She lifted full lips parted invitingly.

The thought of that kiss could still fill him with a sweet,
aching sensation. He could smell the musky fragrance she wore
and feel the heat of her body pressed against his.

He never understood why she left to visit her aunt two weeks
later. He wrote to her every day for the month she was there. It
was after her return that his father called him into his study.

"Deverell, I do not know how to say this, my boy, but Ariadne's father has just left the house. He came to tell me that she
is going to marry Edward Barrington, Viscount of Chatham."

Deverell's face blanched, then flushed. He could not speak.
He turned on his heel and left the room.

"Deverell. Dev!" his father called, but he ran down the hall
and out of the house to the stable. He ignored the groom and
the stable boy and saddled his horse himself. He mounted the
gelding and prodded him into a gallop. They tore from the yard
into the open meadow.

When he came to the woods, he slowed his mount and
slumped over in the saddle like a man with the wind knocked
out of him. Edward Barrington was twice Ariadne's age and a
cold fish, but he had something Deverell could never give her:
a title. She'd be a viscountess. Lady Chatham. His own family
was in trade. Evidently love didn't matter if you could be a
viscountess. He had never allowed anyone to talk about her
since, nor did he speak her name again.

The first year he was filled with anger at Ariadne's treachery.
No woman, he vowed, would own his heart again. He involved
himself in the family business and spent time with a few good
friends. His poor mother despaired of his ever finding a wife.
He rarely thought of Ariadne anymore, and if he did, it was
with detachment.

Somehow Alexi had breached the walls he had built around

his life. She had taken him by surprise, and he was vulnerable again. Dash it all, he would not let her throw his comfortable life into chaos. He picked up the pen and wrote.

> *Dear Miss Moreton,*
> *I have seen your brother, and I am afraid your assessment of the situation is accurate. I shall stay in touch with him, but I am not sure I will have any influence.*
> *Please let me know if there is anything more I can do.*
> *Your servant,*
> *Deverell Bromfield*

Alexi received Deverell's letter from her maid. He must have talked to Lucian already. Disappointed that her brother was so hardheaded, she was, nonetheless, delighted that Deverell had acted promptly. She penned her thanks.

Maybe he was still that caring person she had known years ago. Alexi sighed. She loved the way his eyes lit up when he saw her. Would he still feel the same if he knew she was the rider who almost ran him down . . . twice?

Chapter Six

"Mary," Leticia called from the top of the stairs. "Mary, where are you? You're never around when I need you."

"Yes, miss." Mary stood in the arched doorway of the small dining room and held the breakfast tray in her hands.

Her mistress stomped one slipper-clad foot. "At last." Leticia puckered her mouth in a pout.

"You were sleeping the last time I looked in, miss."

"Fielding is coming for dinner tonight, and I want to do some shopping before he arrives."

At the top of the steps Mary stopped to catch her breath, her face red with exertion.

"What dress shall I put out for you, Miss Leticia?"

"My pink muslin for today with the burgundy pelisse, and for tonight the blue silk with the navy spencer. Blue is Fielding's favorite color. Did he have the food sent in for dinner?"

"Yes, miss. The makings for a fine meal arrived early this morning. There'll be 'am and veal pie, soup with asparagus tips, sole à la Colbert, and whipped syllabub."

Leticia pushed open the door to her boudoir. "Is Daisy here to help you in the kitchen?"

"Yes, miss." Mary set the tray on the table by the window and pulled the chair out.

"I wonder what surprise he has for me. I hope he is taking me out to a play or the opera. How I wish I could go to Almack's."

"'E can't take you there, miss."

"Why not? The Prince Regent takes his mistress there."

Leticia sat down, picked up the toast, and spread some jam on it.

"Mr. Stanhope is not the Prince Regent. 'E's not even aristocracy."

"Yes, that is a disadvantage." She sighed. "Why isn't he a duke or at least a baron? I would be able to go out on the town."

"'E is very rich, Miss Leticia. And if I may be so bold, 'e is a lot better than your last situation."

"Do not remind me of that drunken sot. You may go. I want to eat my breakfast."

She poured herself a cup of tea. How could she persuade Fielding to take her out more? He didn't understand the needs of a highly social young lady. She had friends who came to visit her, but she wanted to be seen and admired at Almack's and in the salons at Bath.

Later Mary came back to help her dress and do her hair.

"You'd think Fielding would give me a small carriage to have at my disposal. It's so inconvenient to use a hackney every time I want to go out," Leticia said as she smoothed her dress over her hips.

Mary fastened the buttons and tied the ribbon at her waist. "'E gives you pocket money for all your expenses, miss."

Leticia frowned. "You always take his side, Mary. You should be more concerned for me."

Mary lifted her eyebrows. "I am thinking about you, miss. 'E treats you well, and 'e puts up with your flirtations."

"You sound like my mother."

"Yes, miss." Mary pulled out the vanity stool and helped Leticia straighten her dress so it wouldn't wrinkle as she sat down.

The woman brushed her hair into long golden curls, then caught them up in ribbons on each side of Leticia's face.

Mary set the bonnet with the pink feathers on the back of Leticia's head and tied the ribbons at the side of her chin. "You look lovely, miss." She gave her mistress the hand mirror and watched with a smile as Leticia arranged an errant blond curl.

"Go find a hackney for me, Mary," she said with a wave of her hand.

About ten minutes later Leticia heard Mary's call. "The cab is out front, miss."

"Thank you, Mary," she said as she sailed through the door. "Take me to Fleet Street, please," Leticia told the coachman. She would buy ribbons and flowers to brighten her old bonnet, but first she would get Fielding a silk lounging robe. He would be pleased with her. Maybe he would take her to Bath for a holiday.

The ride through the narrow streets was slow and tedious in the lumbering old coach. Leticia sat by the window and held a handkerchief to her nose, for the London air was full of soot and pungent smells. Throngs of people walked casually in front of the shops, looking at the yards of fabric, jewelry, and dishes displayed in the large glass windows.

The hackney stopped in front of Shudall's. The coachman opened the door for her and offered his hand. She pressed a coin into it.

Leticia knew a young woman should not be out in public without her abigail, but Mary was busy with dinner.

A well-dressed gentleman held the door open, and she gave him her most devastating smile.

"May I help you, madame?" asked a wizened clerk with white hair and wrinkles etched at the sides of his turned-down mouth.

"I am looking for a silk lounging robe for my father. Medium blue with a navy stripe would be just the thing."

"His size, please."

"Size? Oh, yes, of course." How would she know that?

"Look around and see if you find someone his height and girth," suggested the clerk.

"Miss Browning?"

She felt a tap on her shoulder.

She turned and looked into the face of a tall gentleman.

"Lord Brendan Helmsley at your service, ma'am. I'm a friend of Stanhope's."

"I remember. You were at his last party." She held out her hand. He took it and lightly kissed her fingers. He was handsome with nice manners.

The clerk coughed.

"I am sorry, I've kept you waiting. Lord Helmsley, could you help me find a lounging robe for my father?" She turned her head so the brim of her bonnet hid her face from the clerk and winked at Brendan. "You know him."

"It would be my pleasure. I shop here often and believe I can help you find something suitable." He raised an eyebrow as he looked around the store.

He strode to a table in the front of the shop and picked up a brown robe trimmed with ivory. "This is his size."

"I believe he would prefer the blue one."

Lord Brendan picked up the blue one and handed it to the clerk.

"Put it in something suitable for a gift, please," said Leticia.

"Yes, miss." He took the robe to the back of the store to wrap.

"Miss Browning, shall I call your coach?" asked Lord Helmsley.

Leticia dropped her gaze, allowing her long lashes to sweep her cheeks. "That is kind of you, but I came in a hackney." A soft sigh escaped her lips as she looked at him.

"A hackney! Stanhope lets you flit about town in a hackney?"

Leticia felt her cheeks warm, and she hoped they had pinked up nicely. She shrugged and gave him a half smile.

"My coach is right outside. I would be honored if you would let me carry you across town." His eyes held hers, and his voice intimated more than a carriage ride.

"I would be delighted, Lord Helmsley." The sides of her mouth lifted in a smile. A title, a coach, and a roguish look. She was *sure* there was a promise of more.

Lord Helmsley handed her into his Berlin with the family crest on the door in gold, then took the seat facing her. Their knees touched.

Her package and reticule secure in her lap, she leaned back against the squabs and luxuriated in the well-sprung coach. She lifted her long lashes to gaze into his dark, flirtatious eyes.

The next morning a nosegay of violets and a note from Lord Helmsley arrived for Leticia.

Chapter Seven

It was nice of your mother to send these lovely pears. Come into the kitchen, and we'll cut some up."

Deverell followed Alexi through the house. He noticed how the deep green riding habit fit her becoming curves and how the feather on her hat brushed against her cheek. He wondered how it would feel to brush his fingers against her skin.

"I don't want to keep you from your ride." He brought his thoughts back to the moment.

"Don't be silly. I can go later." Alexi pushed open the door to the kitchen and set the basket of pears on the table. Cutting two of the sun-kissed fruits into wedges, she placed them on a platter.

"Shall we take these outside to Mother?"

Deverell took the platter and followed her onto the terrace to find Mrs. Moreton resting on a chaise lounge.

"See what Deverell brought us, Mother." Alexi set the tray on the table beside the chaise and took a chair.

"How kind—your mother knows they're my favorite. Please, sit down."

Alexi picked up one of the pieces of pear and bit into it. "Mmm, juicy and sweet," she said as she licked her fingers.

Deverell's mouth twitched.

"I know it's not proper etiquette," said Alexandra, with a mischievous grin.

"They are wonderful. Please have some," Mrs. Moreton insisted. She pushed the platter toward Deverell. "The weather is so inviting, why don't the two of you take a ride?"

Deverell stood and offered his arm to Alexi. "Would you like that?"

"Very much."

They took the stone path to the stables. "When you saw Lucian, how did he look?" she asked.

"Tired, worn around the edges. I think he misses his family. He didn't look happy."

Alexandra brushed her hand across her eyes. "Thank you for seeing him."

In front of the stables the groom, Bobby, held the bridle of a fine-looking mare.

"She is a beauty, Mr. Bromfield," Alexandra said, admiring the lines of his horse.

"Yes, I've had Queen Bess about a year." He rubbed the horse's nose as she nuzzled him.

Alexandra took a carrot from her pocket, broke it in half, and offered it to the mare.

Deverell detected the fragrance of lavender as she stood close to him. He had noticed that scent before, but where?

The horse curled back her lips and took the morsel from Alexi's fingers.

Out of the corner of his eye Deverell saw Alexi furtively motion to a stable boy who stood in the doorway, a large bay standing saddled behind him. She seemed to be telling him to go away, and the boy wore a puzzled look.

"Bobby, have Franny saddled for me, please." Alexi's voice had a frantic note.

"Get Franny for the mistress, Jem," the groom called to the bewildered boy.

Alexi! He should have known. The hair. The impudence. The lavender scent. The bay gelding. Clever girl, she'd fooled him completely. Well, he'd find a way to return the favor. "I'm sorry. What did you say?" Deverell asked.

"Are you prepared to ride?" Alexi's eyes challenged him.

He lifted his chin. "I am."

When a puzzled Jem had brought Franny, they rode off together, the groom several paces behind.

"I'll race you to the hedges." Alexi nudged her horse into a gallop.

Surprised, Deverell urged his horse to catch up. Would she try to jump those hedges?

He caught up with her as she neared them. She turned her horse. Her cheeks rosy from the brisk air, she announced, "I beat you, Mr. Bromfield."

"By inches, my dear Miss Moreton, and I like it better when you call me Deverell."

"Would that be proper, sir?"

"'Pon rep, I have known you since you were a scrawny child, as you were quick to remind me. Surely we can call each other by our first names, at least in private."

"The word was *gangly,* and I agree. You shall be Dev, and I, Alexi."

Deverell's mare sidled up beside hers. They dismounted and walked their horses along the hedge.

Alexandra asked, "Are you planning on breeding your filly when she comes of age? My father just purchased a grand stallion. I am sure he would let you use him."

Deverell grinned broadly. He asked, "Do you think that is proper conversation for a young woman and her male escort?"

"Please, my father has raised horses since before I was born. I have spent a great deal of time in the stables. I've watched more than one foal born. Although my mother never approved."

"I'm sure she did not. That is probably one of the reasons she sent you off to the Académie for Young Ladies."

"I am a physician's daughter. I've read several of his medical books, and more than once I've heard my father and his colleagues discuss their patients."

"Really? Did they know you were listening?"

Alexandra blushed to her hair roots. "Well, not exactly."

"Eavesdropping?" He lifted an eyebrow in mock astonishment.

"How is a girl to find out anything if she does not listen? No one will tell you about love or marriage or having children. It is all so mysterious. I think it's terrible the way women come to marriage without an idea of what is expected beyond being a good hostess and compliant wife."

"You are serious."

Her cheeks flushed again. "Yes, I am. I have a friend who married at sixteen, and by twenty she had three children and was pregnant with the fourth. She nearly died in childbirth, but my father saved her life."

She looked at Deverell, and he could see the frustration in her eyes. There was so much more than a pretty face to this woman. She cared about people.

"I had my father's medical books to educate me. It took my mother a long time to discover where I found the information for all the questions I asked her."

His smile was gentle. "I am sure she did not approve of you reading them."

She turned her head away. "I've done it again. I forgot myself. My mother has told me I overstep the bounds of propriety. You must think me a . . . a . . ."

"Please, look at me, Alexi."

He turned her chin gently toward him, brushing one finger over her cheek. When she looked up at him, his heart seemed to stop and then pound in his chest. She lifted her face, and her lips invited his kiss.

But icy blue eyes replaced sea-green ones, and auburn hair turned to blond in his mind. Deverell dropped his hand as if he had been burned

In flustered silence the two mounted their horses and turned toward home.

Alexi couldn't believe she'd almost let Deverell kiss her.

"Tired?" Deverell drew up beside her.

"It's time to go home. I have several things I need to do." Beneath the broad brim of his new topper she could see his set jaw and mouth. They rode home in a fulminating silence.

Mrs. Moreton bustled out of the sunroom when she heard voices in the hall. "That was a short ride."

"Quite," said Alexi.

"I thought you might like some lunch before you started home, Deverell. I hope I was not too presumptuous." Mrs. Moreton smiled wistfully.

"Not at all. It is most thoughtful." He took her arm and walked with her to the sunroom, where a small table was set for three.

The meal was quiet except for the occasional questions from Mrs. Moreton, which were answered politely by Deverell and in monosyllables by Alexi.

When the meal was finished and Deverell stood to take his leave, Mrs. Moreton said, "Thank your mother for the delicious pears, and send her my regards. Alexi, walk him out to the entry, please."

At the door he turned to her. A smile lifted the corners of his mouth when he said, "Next time you ride the bay, please be more careful." He took her hand and bowed over it, but his lips barely touched her fingertips. He closed the door before she could reply.

All the way home from the Moretons' Deverell chastised himself. He had almost kissed Alexi. What was he thinking? "Well, Queen Bess, a fine muddle I've gotten myself into." He patted her neck.

The horse twitched her ears and tossed her head.

"She's beautiful and fun but serious as well. Is she a child or a woman? Every time I seem to make up my mind, the specter of Ariadne rises."

"Tea is about to be served. Sit here by me," Alexi's mother said.

"Would you like me to pour, ma'am?" The maid set the tray on a table.

"No, thank you, Emmy. You may go." Mrs. Moreton offered Alexi some cucumber sandwiches.

"Is there anything you would like to tell me about you and Deverell Bromfield, Alexandra?"

"What do you mean, Mama?" She'd almost let him kiss her. In truth, she'd wanted him to, and when he didn't, she was angry. *You still like him, you dunce.*

"Don't be coy with me, dear." She smiled. "You were never able to dissemble. I know you had a fondness for him when you were an adolescent. Have the passing years dimmed its luster?"

"Mama, I have made such a mess of things." She told her about the two disastrous rides on the bay. "I know it was foolish, but being ladylike is so boring."

Isabel wanted to shake the girl. Would she never grow up? But when she saw the tears running down Alexi's cheeks, she opened her arms and drew her daughter in.

Alexi brushed the tears away and whispered, "One moment I am angry with him, the next I'm confused. Once he was my hero; now I don't know. To make it worse, he acts like he cares for me, and then he treats me like a child."

"Alexandra, I think we need a change of scene, maybe a shopping trip to London. We could stay in the town house for a few weeks. I am sure your father would be glad of the company. A dinner party might be in order as well. I'll try to see Lucian, and I am sure you could find something to keep you from getting bored."

"Mama, I think you're right. There are all kinds of possibilities. When shall we leave?"

"As soon as possible."

Over the next two days at the Moreton home a flurry of packing prevailed. On the third day after a light luncheon, the two ladies and their maids were ensconced in the coach. Their trunks were tied to the back and in another smaller vehicle to follow.

"Alexi, I can hardly believe we were able to get everything together so quickly. We could never have done it without the help of Abby and Sophy."

The two maids smiled. "Thank you, ma'am," they chorused.

Alexi fell against her mother as the coach hit another pothole. "These roads are pockmarked with holes the size of a pony," she said as her bonnet brushed against the top of the landau.

"Your father says this coach is well-sprung, but I will be thankful when it's time to stop for tea."

Abby moaned, "I hope I shall not be sick, miss, with all this swaying and jolting about."

"Lay your head back and try to nap," said Alexi.

Abby answered with a soft groan.

Several hours later the coach arrived at their town home near the East End. Mrs. Moreton said, "I am sure your father is still in his office. We'll go directly upstairs so as not to disturb him. Come to my room when you have freshened up, Alexi."

"I'll be there shortly."

A few minutes later she knocked on her mother's door. "I love this room with its yellow walls and white-painted furniture, Mama."

Her mother looked around the room. "It is cheerful."

There were footsteps outside the door, and Dr. Moreton could be heard talking to the footman who was delivering the trunks. Isabel rose and waited by the bed for her husband to enter.

He kissed his wife's cheek. "Mrs. Moreton, why didn't you tell me you were coming, and you too, Alexandra? I am pleased to see you both."

"We thought we would surprise you. We were getting bored at home and have come to do some shopping."

"Ah, you are going to flatten my purse, no doubt. No matter; it is good to have you here. I am sure we can find something to entertain you. I have one more patient, and then I shall be up to dress for dinner."

They looked at a rainbow of fabric and laces and ribbons. The footman staggered beneath the growing stack of boxes and packages as he followed them through the shops.

"Mama, we have had two wonderful days of shopping in Leicester Square. I am most eager to have dresses made from the fabrics we purchased. Do you think the seamstress your friend recommended will be able to make up the dresses as well as our own Mrs. Beadle?"

"I'm sure of it, Alexandra. Mrs. Cornellis is always dressed in the height of fashion. We shall take the fabrics to her seamstress tomorrow, and she can help us pick out the patterns."

"A small dinner party will show off our finery and dazzle Papa with how well we have spent his money. Would we dare go to the opera too?"

"Good idea. A week from Friday, I think. We shall write our invitations when we get back from the seamstress. The Bromfields will be in town then also. I heard from Anne Louise this morning." Isabel smiled at her daughter.

"Mama, you are planning something."

"Never."

Chapter Eight

Deverell's feelings for Alexi chafed like a pair of ill-fitting boots. He could not get her out of his mind: her mischievous ways, the smile that lit up her eyes, the passion she had for things she felt strongly about. She was wrapped around his heart by a hundred threads, but could he trust a woman again? Tonight he would have another chance to find out. He would make the most of it. He suspected his mother's hand in the invitation to join the Moretons at the opera. She had made it clear she liked Alexi.

After pulling his knee breeches on and smoothing the white stockings over his calves, he tucked in his white fine linen shirt. He manipulated his white neck cloth into an elegant knot and buttoned his embroidered silk waistcoat.

A soft knock announced Chess. "I will help you with your coat, sir. Your father is dressed and waiting downstairs."

Chess eased the coat onto Deverell's arms, pulling it gently over his shoulders. He smoothed the back and made sure the tails hung properly, then handed Deverell his gloves and ebony cane.

Deverell smiled at the man he had known since Deverell was a boy. "Thank you. I won't carry the cane tonight, Chess. I shall take the quizzing glass instead." He pulled on his gloves.

Chess took the small glass ornament out of its box and hung it around Deverell's neck.

"Planning to give someone a set down, sir?"

"One never knows what the evening holds." Deverell held the glass to his eye.

"You are looking well, if I may say so, sir, a fine figure. Reminds me of your father in his younger years."

"Thank you, Chess. You couldn't give me a better compliment."

Deverell joined his father downstairs. "Are we picking up the Moretons, or will they meet us at the opera?"

"We will meet them there. Ah, here is your mother now. You look lovely, my dear," he said as he put her evening cape around her shoulders.

Deverell held the door while the two older couples entered the box of the opera house. Alexi whispered as Dev took her arm, "This box is reserved by a patient of my father's, and he lent it to him for this evening. We've never had a box before."

He led her to one of the red upholstered seats behind the front row. Her lavender scent tantalized his nose, and he leaned closer. The thought of placing a kiss on the curve of her neck flitted through his mind.

"We won't be able to see from here," she protested.

"It won't matter. The diva is getting too old to play romantic leads, and the bass wears a corset to hold in his paunch, although how he can possibly sing with one squeezing his middle is beyond my imagination. You can rest assured, we will be able to hear. The soprano shatters glass with her high C."

Alexi's soft giggle delighted him.

"You are impossible," she said. "I perceive you are not enchanted by the opera."

"Only by the lovely lady who sits next to me."

She looked up at him. A slight smile curved her lips. "You are very kind, Mr. Bromfield."

His eyes held hers, and he laid his hand gently upon her arm. His gaze slid down over her nose to a faint scattering of freckles. He'd never noticed those before. Then he looked at her lips. He *had* noticed them.

He saw Alexi blush as though she had read his mind.

The orchestra began the overture, and she turned to watch

the stage. Deverell settled into his seat, but he did not remove his hand from her arm. The warmth of her skin through his glove sent a tantalizing rush through him. He wondered if she felt it as well.

At intermission they bought glasses of punch and wandered through the crowded lobby. A tall young man with blond hair curled across his brow walked toward them.

"Bromfield, haven't seen you in a while," said Lord Helmsley.

Deverell saw the way the man eyed Alexandra. His hand clenched into a fist as he felt anger bubble up inside. The rake. He would have preferred to give him the cut, but good manners prevented it. He raised his quizzing glass.

"Ah, yes, Lord Helmsley, how do you do?"

"Quite well, if I do say so." He smiled at Alexi. "Aren't you going to introduce me, Bromfield?"

"Miss Alexandra Moreton, Lord Brendan Helmsley."

Helmsley took her hand and bowed low over it. "Charmed, I must say."

Alexi gave him a slight nod and lifted one corner of her mouth in a half smile.

"If you'll excuse us now, we must be getting back to our box." Deverell took Alexi's hand, tucked it beneath his arm, and turned on his heel.

"Who was that?" Alexi asked when they were out of earshot. "He might be handsome if his eyes weren't so appraising."

"Someone I would rather not acknowledge in the society of a lady."

"I gathered that, but why?"

"The man is a duke's son and feels himself above the laws of society." His irritation showed in the tone of his voice.

"Oh?" She raised an eyebrow.

"Many women have fallen under the spell of his noble birth and money, only to be broken by him. If you don't mind, I would rather change the subject."

"Gladly. Would it be possible for me to see your textile mill, Dev?"

Surprised, he looked down at her. "Are you sure you really

want to? Have you ever been in that area of London? It's quite poverty-stricken."

"Briefly once, when Mother and I were lost, but our coach-man hurried us off the street."

"If you come, you should borrow a dress and a cloak from your lady's maid and a bonnet too. You will need to bring her as well. I'll come for you in our coach, as it is familiar to the people in the neighborhood, and they respect my father."

"You're certainly taking a lot of precautions," said Alexandra. She stopped and turned to him.

"The poor people of London live desperate and hopeless lives, and they are often driven to extreme behavior. They resent the rich, whom they see as the ones that keep them poor. It can be dangerous in such sections of town."

Alexi shivered. "I see that I know very little of life outside my own circle."

"I assure you, I'll keep you safe, if you would still like to come."

"I would."

"I shall arrange it, with your parents' permission. Now we had better get back to our box." He took her arm and led her up the grand staircase.

A few days later the Bromfield carriage drew up to the Moreton home. The door of the house opened, and three young women swarmed out as Deverell stepped down. He bowed to the ladies. "What is this?" he asked Alexi.

"I mentioned the mill to my friend, Caroline Witherspoon, and she was interested as well, so I invited her to come along with Abby and me. I hope that is all right."

"It is very nice to meet you, Miss Witherspoon. I see you all have taken my advice and dressed simply." He smiled at the ladies and offered Alexi a hand up into the seat.

"Tell us about the textile mill, Mr. Bromfield," said Caroline when they were all seated comfortably.

"We weave very fine cotton there like you buy for your muslin dresses."

"Has your family been in the textile business long?" Caroline asked.

Sitting forward, he said, "My father learned the trade from a gentleman who owned a mill in a town near our home in Midfield. But my father did not like the man's practice of bringing in children from the workhouses and working them long hours in unhealthy conditions."

"Children? You use children in the textile mill?" asked Alexi, a frown wrinkling her brow.

"We do. But my father believed he could build a better mill in London, where there were plenty of willing laborers. He found an old building in an industrial part of town with small neighborhoods of people living around it. He and Mother put together all the money they had and bought the empty warehouse. It was refurbished inside and out. They built a dining room in it and two small classrooms."

"Classrooms?" asked Alexi, interest in her face.

He turned to her with a smile. "Yes, all the children are taught to read, write, and do sums. Adults are also encouraged to take the classes."

"I have read that the children taken from the workhouses often sign a contract that they will work in the mill until they are twenty-one," said Caroline.

"That's true; they are called 'pauper apprentices.' Michael Sadler and Lord Ashley have been working in the House of Commons to improve their plight. My father has always believed in treating his employees well, and he has been ostracized in some circles because of it. They say they cannot make money if they work the children fewer hours and provide proper ventilation and working conditions. He has proven them wrong."

Deverell looked out the window. "We are entering the area now."

They looked out at houses that were little more than shacks built side by side with no yards between.

"There is a small lot of dirt in the back, and some are able to grow a few vegetables to add to their meager diet," said Deverell.

"Oh, my, there is no place for the children to play," said Caroline.

"They have little time to play here. They work, have a few hours of school, and help their parents. It is not an easy life for a child," said Deverell.

"It is not an easy life for anyone," said Alexi. Her voice showed her distress. She drew their attention to a young woman coming out of one of the hovels. Her patched dress hung on her scrawny frame. Hardly more than a girl herself, she held a baby on her hip and a toddler with her other hand.

The coachman slowed the horses. They pulled in front of a large building painted white with the name BROMFIELD TEX-TILES in black across the side. The party entered through a small side door.

"I will take you to my office and then into the dining area upstairs. There you will have a good view of the looms below through the large panes of glass in the wall."

The group met Edgar and looked briefly into Deverell's small, untidy office before they continued down the hallway to the steps.

"What are those machines called? Good grief, there are children under them!" Alexi, her expression anxious, pointed to the floor below.

"Those are spinning mules, and the children are rag-gatherers. They remove the rags tangled in the machinery, and when the machines are at rest, they clean the mechanism. We are look-ing for a better way to do this job, but we have found nothing yet." He pointed to some women working at one of the mules. "The women working there are piecers, and they reunite the broken threads."

Deverell led them to the stairs going down into the mill it-self. "Put a hanky over your face. The fluff in the air from the cotton can make you cough. It will be noisy, so we will stay for only a moment or two."

Deverell smiled and spoke to several of the workers, calling them by name.

When they reached the outside door, Alexi was sneezing, and Caroline coughed gently into her hanky.

"How do they get used to the air?" asked Alexi.

"In time they seem to acclimate, although some have trouble with their lungs. We allow the children to have their lessons in the middle of the day, and we only work adults ten hours, including their lunch. Since we do not have to house them, we still make a fair profit."

"Thank you for allowing us to come. It certainly does give one a lot to think about," said Caroline.

"Thank you, Deverell," said Alexi as he climbed into the coach behind her. She was silent for most of the ride home, a thoughtful look upon her face.

They neared the Moretons' home, and she turned to Deverell. "Mother is expecting us for tea; I hope you will be able to stay."

"I would like that."

After tea Deverell took Alexandra out into the small garden. "You were quiet on the ride back. May I ask what were your thoughts?"

"This afternoon opened my mind to how others live. My heart aches to help that mother and those children."

"I know it is overwhelming at first. There are so many needs, but I am sure you will think of some way to help in time."

Her smile lit up her eyes. "Thank you for believing I can do something to improve their lives. We will be going back to the country on Friday. Mother is growing tired of the city."

"I shall be going home too. Stanhope is having one of his parties, and I understand Nat has been spending too much time at his house." Deverell shook his head. "Stanhope is my friend, but he and his cronies are an abysmal influence on my brother. No doubt I'll have to rescue him from some disgraceful escapade again."

Chapter Nine

"Stop making a cake of yourself," said Deverell to Nathaniel. "You can't possibly think that a woman like Leticia Browning is interested in calf-love. She is merely flirting with you."

"She isn't like that!" exclaimed Nat. "Just because she's a friend of Stanhope, who, I admit, is shockingly loose in the haft, doesn't mean she is."

Exasperation showed in every line of Deverell's face. He turned and strode toward the house.

No matter what Deverell said, Nat would dance with Leticia tonight at Stanhope's.

Nat dressed in his black trousers and white shirt with the high pointed collar. He carefully tousled his curly brown hair and adjusted his cravat. He did not want to look the dandy, so he'd chosen a simple knot. The pale yellow waistcoat looked well with his dark blue superfine. He would make an impression on her. One side of his mouth lifted in a lopsided grin as he thought of holding the beautiful Miss Browning.

When Fredrick Bromfield came down for supper and found his wife alone on the sofa, he asked, "Where are our sons this evening?"

Anna Louise thought how handsome he looked with his side-whiskers turning gray and his figure still youthful. There was a glow of love and pride in her when he walked into the room. She patted the seat beside her, inviting him to sit down for a moment.

"They are both at Fielding Stanhope's, my dear."

"Another one of his parties, I suppose," he said as he sat down, putting his feet upon the hassock and relaxing against the pillows. He reached over to take her hand. "I am glad to see that Nat has gone as well. He spends entirely too much time at home. I wish the boy would decide what he is going to do. I can't interest him in anything at the mill."

She leaned closer. "I don't think he likes the city, dear. He seems to prefer the rural life."

"I doubt he'll make much money in the country. He'll have to learn to make his own way, you know. A man must make a living. I have always tried to be an example to our boys."

"That's true," she observed, "and you've created a fine business and taken good care of us." She paused. "I was wondering if you could spend a little more time with the boys, since things are going so well at the mill."

"They're men now. You must remember that."

"I know, but they still need their father to give them guidance," she said.

"I do spend a great deal of time with Deverell, my dear. He'll do a fine job someday when I retire."

"I was thinking of Nat. It seems there's a girl at this party he's attracted to. I'm afraid she may not be the right sort. Esmerelda has never given a thought to what Fielding does or who his friends are."

"You forget that Deverell is one of Stanhope's closest friends. Although I do not totally approve of him myself, I don't see that he's overly influenced Deverell."

"Nat's much younger and more easily led, I fear. I'd take it most kindly if you'd talk to him," she said with a winsome smile.

They both stood as the maid came to announce dinner.

"Of course, my love." He smiled at her with deep fondness as he took her arm and led her into the dining room. "Did I tell you how becoming you look in that yellow dress?"

Nat waited until he heard his brother ride off before he went to get his horse. The filly, a birthday gift from his father, was a beautiful, high-spirited chestnut. From the door of her stall

Lady whinnied when Nat held out a carrot to her. Ears perked forward, she blew softly and took the treat daintily from his hand. He led her out into the yard, where the stable boy gave him a hand up. An evening of dancing and flirting lay ahead— what a night it would be. A low chuckle became a full-throated laugh as he gave the horse her head.

He'd avoid Deverell on the ride to Stanhope's. He didn't relish pulling caps again as they had this afternoon. No sense getting into a snit with such a wonderful night ahead. He hardly noticed the moonlight filtering through the leaves of the trees and speckling the road through the orchard to Stanhope's home.

Nat's heart raced as he anticipated the feel of Leticia's soft hand in his. The look in her eyes and the wink and smile she gave him the last time they danced still made his stomach churn. She was a few years older than he was, but that only made her more desirable.

Stanhope's windows glowed brightly, and several horses and curricles stood in front of the house. Nat dismounted and gave the reins to one of the stable boys waiting nearby.

"I would like her in the stable, please."

"Yes, sir," replied the boy.

The door opened, and a young man stepped out onto the porch. Nat ran up the stairs, and the young man leaned unsteadily against the wall, lighting a cigar. Nat inhaled the pungent smell as he passed. Music and loud laughter assailed his ears as he entered the hall, where the butler took his coat. He took the stairs to the drawing room that was lit by wall sconces and a large chandelier. Thank goodness Stanhope's parties were never formal affairs. There were chairs around the walls and a long table filled with food at one end of the room. Esmerelda Stanhope and a few of her friends were playing cards in a far corner. He supposed they were the chaperones for the evening. Many of the young bucks were gathered around the table where alcohol was being poured. He didn't hold his liquor well, so he rarely drank. His gaze scoured the room, looking for a certain blond with the face of an angel.

A laugh behind him caused him to turn. It was Leticia.

Mesmerized by the vision of her well-rounded figure in a white silk dress, he smiled and bowed. With a slight nod and a charming wink, she acknowledged him. The low-cut bodice revealed her white bosom hiding behind a row of lace, and the skirt gracefully clung to her body as she moved.

Stanhope took her arm and swept her onto the dance floor as the musicians began to play. The soft skirt of her dress rose and dipped occasionally, showing her dainty feet and even a brief glimpse of an ankle encased in a white silk stocking. Nat reluctantly withdrew his gaze from the dance floor and looked around for some young men his age. Seeing no one he knew, he stood by the wall until he could ask Miss Browning for a dance.

Deverell sidled up beside him and said, "I see you have come, little brother. Please try not to disgrace yourself tonight. She's really not for you."

Nat flushed and started to retort, when his brother laid his hand on his arm and said, "Don't let us bandy words. I'm giving you some brotherly advice, that's all." With that Deverell walked away, leaving Nat to fume.

"I need something to drink," Nat said under his breath.

With a glass of wine in his hand Nat watched the dancers until the music ended and Stanhope left Leticia on the other side of the room.

Nat put the empty glass on a table and pushed his way through a small group of men and women to Miss Browning's side.

"Good evening," he said in his deepest voice.

Leticia raised her long, thick lashes, slowly revealing remarkable blue-violet eyes. Nat blushed. She smiled at him.

"Did you want to dance with me, Mr. B?" she asked boldly.

"I would be delighted, ma'am," he answered, his heart beating faster.

"Then I shall save the next one for you." Giving him a quick curtsy, she floated away.

His mind on holding Leticia in his arms, he paid little attention to anything else as he waited for the musicians to start the next dance. He was at her side when Stanhope took her arm to lead her onto the floor.

Kaye Calkins

"This dance has been spoken for," said Leticia.

Stanhope's face flushed with anger as she turned away and took Nat's arm.

Stanhope stood on the sidelines watching them. Deverell approached him. "Don't worry about my little brother. She's teasing him because he's such an easy mark."

"I don't mind telling you, Bromfield, I wish your brother at Jericho." Stanhope ran his fingers through his dark hair, pushing it off his forehead. "You haven't brought the lovely Alexandra tonight."

"To one of your parties? You must be joking. Come, let's find something to drink. Leticia will be done with Nat soon enough," cajoled Deverell.

Nat's pulse raced. Every moment he was beside her was magic; the touch of her hand sent heat coursing through his veins. Reluctantly he released her hand at the end of the dance.

He moved to the wall where he could watch her across the room. A tall blond man with his cravat tied in a *Trone d'Amour* and a coat from Weston's found his way to Nat's side. "I see you've been dancing with the beautiful Miss Browning. I'm surprised Stanhope would allow you to dance with his *incognita*. He keeps her close to his side," said Lord Helmsley.

Nat turned to the man, his face red with anger and his voice low. "You take back that insult to Miss Browning, sir, or I swear I shall plant you a facer."

"Oh, that's the way the land lies, is it? Well, I have no intention of denying the truth, sir. She'll go with the highest bidder. It's best you know it now before you get in too deep."

"I'll be waiting for you outside, and if you're not there in three minutes, I'll put it about you're a coward," said Nat between clenched teeth.

"I'll be there, my boy; you can depend on it," Helmsley said with a chuckle.

Some of the other guests overheard their heated conversation. One of them spoke with a malicious grin. "That young man's in for a surprise. Helmsley may look like a dandy, but he displays to advantage. He's beaten quite a few men with his bare hands."

Outside, the men sparred. Nat threw wild punches in his anger, and Hemsley waited for his opportunity. Nat never saw the uppercut that put him to sleep.

Deverell watched Lucian Moreton cross the room and stop beside him. "I think you had better go outside and tend to your brother," Lucian told him. "Take a pitcher of water with you."

"Oh, fustian, what has that skitter-brain done now?"

The boy lay at the bottom of the steps. Deverell spilled the pitcher of water on him and helped him sit up. Dazed, Nat couldn't focus his eyes.

Deverell called the stable hand. "Bring our horses. I shall be right back."

When the hand returned, it took both of them to put Nat on his horse. Deverell mounted and rode beside the stunned boy.

"Even though Stanhope is my friend, I do not approve of his parties and the people with whom he surrounds himself. Please, Nat, trust me."

Nat grunted at him and put his hand to his swelling jaw.

Deverell could see the humiliation written all over his brother's face. There'd be a purple bruise on the boy's chin in the morning. Dev hoped his parents would be in bed when they arrived home.

Chapter Ten

How dare he treat her like this? Leticia thought on her way back to London the next day. She couldn't help it if some love-struck puppy got into a fight over her. She hadn't provoked it.

Bumped and thrown from side to side in Stanhope's carriage, she straightened her dark blue bonnet, which was askew. He must have told his driver to take her home as fast as the road allowed. Well, it would take more than some frivolous little bauble to make it up to her this time.

Stanhope was far too possessive and jealous—and over such a harmless flirtation at that.

A tingle crawled up her spine, and her palms suddenly grew wet. What if Fielding found out about the other men who visited when he was not in London?

Nat stretched, then winced when he touched his chin. He pulled himself out of bed and limped to the cheval glass. He must have twisted his ankle when he fell. He put his hand to his throbbing face and felt the lump. A large purple bruise extended across the side of his jaw. His whole body ached. With a grimace, he crawled back into bed and pulled the covers over his head.

He woke sometime later, his belly growling. Could he make it downstairs to the kitchen without his parents catching sight of his face? He put on his dressing gown and opened the door. The upstairs maid was in the hall, sweeping the floor.

"Annie," he called in a low voice.

"Master Nathaniel, is that you?" she asked as he pulled the door closed.

"Could you bring me some breakfast, please?" he said through the door.

"It's past noon, sir, but I can bring you breakfast if that's what you want."

"Lunch will be fine."

After cold beef, bread, and cheese washed down with several cups of tea, he settled against the head of his bed to read. Try as he might to concentrate on the words, though, his thoughts strayed to Leticia. What must she think of him? He hadn't even said good night. How could he see her and explain? The book lay on the bed as his mind filled with the music and the softness and warmth of Leticia in his arms. He drifted off to sleep again.

The next morning he went out to the stable before his mother was up. He planned to ride Lady and avoid people if possible. At the stable door he heard Deverell and Stanhope inside talking.

"I hoped to catch you before you went off to London this morning. I sent Leticia home to Newbury Court. She was furious with me, but I will not allow a woman to make a fool of herself and me in my own home," said Stanhope, his words clipped and brusque.

Nat hurried around the side of the stable and waited where they could not see him.

The man continued, "Keep your brother away from me, Bromfield."

"Don't worry; he hasn't been out of his room since he came home."

The two men left the stable, Deverell leading his horse.

Stanhope, his voice still angry, said, "He wasn't the only one she was flirting with that night. She disappeared for about a half hour after your brother left."

"I declare, you sound like a jealous lover," Deverell said. He mounted his horse.

"I guess I do; sometimes she makes my blood boil." Stanhope motioned to the stable boy to give him a hand up on his gelding.

Deverell laughed. "It's just as well you have sent her home, then. I noticed Lucian Moreton was there the other night. Haven't seen much of him lately." They walked their horses down the drive and out of earshot.

Nat waited until he was sure they couldn't see him, then entered the stable. He waved the stable boy off and gave his horse a carrot to munch while he saddled her. He mounted and rubbed the filly's neck, then turned her toward the meadow where a small stand of elms grew by a stream.

The horse drank from the stream before Nat threw the reins over a low limb of a nearby tree. An old log made a good backrest as he sat on the ground.

It might be weeks before he saw Leticia again. Stanhope wasn't going to invite him to any more of his parties. Leaning his head back, he closed his eyes.

Moments later he opened them and gave a shout. "That's what I'll do!"

Lady lifted her head and snorted.

Stanhope had mentioned where Leticia lived. What was the name of the street? It had something to do with royalty—king, count, court? That was it! Newbury Court. He'd leave for London tomorrow and explain about the fight. When she heard how he had defended her honor, she'd realize he was a man to be reckoned with. The throbbing in his chin sharpened. He rubbed it with care. Even if he'd lost the fight, surely she would be grateful. He'd heard that women felt sorry for a wounded man, especially one injured for their sake.

He stood and reached for the reins of his horse, which nibbled on the grasses around the tree. If he told his parents he was going into town to visit some friends for a few days, it wouldn't be a lie.

His father knocked on the door, and without waiting for an answer, he entered the bedroom. "Going to London, are you,

Nat? I have the names and addresses of a few men you should talk to while you are there." He handed Nat an envelope. "They may be able to find you some worthy employment. How are you fixed for money?"

Nat cleared his throat. "I have my check from Grandfather's trust." He tucked the envelope into his valise and packed a change of shirts and some small clothes. He was glad his father hadn't asked too many questions.

Later he heard a familiar tapping on the door. "Come in, Mother." He knew she'd bring him something to eat for the journey.

She handed him a small parcel. "In case you get hungry on the road, I had Cook make you a little something. You have a bruise on your jaw, son." She touched it gently.

"Thank you." He kissed her cheek. "I shall be fine—just a little bump on the chin." He picked up his valise and, putting an arm around his mother, walked with her down the stairs to the front door, where she kissed him good-bye.

Astride his horse, his valise attached to the back of his saddle, his monthly allowance in his pocket, he was free to think of the beautiful Miss Browning. A pleasant spring day and an exhilarating ride before him—what could be better?

The meadows and orchards of the countryside gave way to the noisy streets of the sprawling city. Nat had to ask several times which part of London Leticia's home was in. He knew he was close but couldn't find the street.

A pie man walked by hawking his wares. The fragrant smell reminded Nat he hadn't eaten in a while. He didn't want to take the time to stop, but maybe the man would know where Leticia's street was. "Can you tell me the way to Newbury Court?"

"Well, guv'nor, it's the next street to your left."

"Is there a stable about?"

"On this 'ere road a ways farther."

"Thank you." Nat tossed the man a ha'penny.

He hadn't noticed the change in the weather. The clouds that came scudding in over the city announced an approaching downpour. He handed the reins of his horse to the hostler at the livery and began the two-block walk to Leticia's house. A block away he felt a large raindrop and then another. A drenching rain descended. He scowled. Drat, he'd arrive bedraggled. Hardly what he'd had in mind when he left home in his best riding breeches and coat. His hessians would be muddied as well. Soon his brown hair lay flat on his forehead, dripping water over his face and down his neck. He found the address and knocked sharply on the door. It took a moment or two before the housekeeper answered.

"Is Miss Browning in, please?"

The woman gave him a disdainful look. "I'll see if she's available, sir. May I ask your name?"

"Tell her Mr. B has come to pay a call." He wished he'd worn his topper. It would have kept his hair dry and made him appear older.

"If you'd like to come in, sir. It'll be a moment."

The maid ascended the stairs and tapped on the open door of her mistress' boudoir. "There's a young man 'ere to see you."

Leticia looked up, and her face brightened.

"'E says his name is Mr. B."

Leticia's face fell. She sat at a small table playing a game of solitaire. "What is he doing here?"

"'E's dripping all over the expensive new rug Mr. Stanhope gave you."

"Oh, I suppose I must see him, but give me a few minutes, and, Mary, stoke up the fire so he can dry out."

Leticia flew around the room, putting away the cards and freshening up.

Even if he was a boy, one must look one's best. There was always something intoxicating about a male who thinks you are wonderful. Besides, she was bored, and he would be a small diversion.

Oblivious to the tastefully decorated surroundings, Nat dried off his hair and face with his handkerchief. Maybe this hadn't been such a good idea. What if she wouldn't see him? Or he might be tongue-tied and make a fool of himself.

"If you'll wait 'ere for a few minutes, she'll see you," the housekeeper said.

"Thank you."

When the woman left the room, Nat noticed a mirror near the stairs. He tried to manage a few curls across his forehead, but his hair was too limp. A charming voice from the top of the steps set his heart thundering in his chest. Leticia stood there in a pink gown. "You may come up now. How very nice to see you."

At the top of the stairs he paused. "I . . . I didn't know if you would see me. I wanted to explain about the other night." He could feel his face flushing like a schoolboy's.

She led him down the hall and into her boudoir. He hesitated at the door. Her smile lit up her eyes. "It's perfectly acceptable for you to come in. The *ton* do it. It's quite proper." Leticia motioned him to a seat on the sofa in front of the fire.

Mary came to the door and asked, "Will that be all for this evening, miss?"

"Would you please bring us some port and a pot of tea and some toast?" She turned to Nat and said, "Here, let me take your coat. We must get it dry, or it will be ruined." She helped him remove it and hung it on a straight chair by the fireplace.

Nat took her hand. "Miss Browning, I've come to apologize for any unpleasantness I may have caused you the other evening. I was only trying to defend your honor and . . . well . . . I am sorry," he ended lamely. He felt water run down the side of his face and wiped it with his handkerchief.

She touched the bruise on his chin. He flinched. "Well, I have to admit, it did cause me some discomfort." Shrugging her shoulders, she continued, "But I am sure it will not amount to much." She took the damp kerchief and laid it on the seat with his jacket. She turned to the sofa and gestured to him to sit beside her. "How did you come to London?"

"I rode. I'll be here for a few days."

"Did you leave your horse out in the storm?" She gestured to the rain beating against the window.

"I left her at the livery down the way." Except for the wet clothes, he felt comfortable before the crackling fire. Sitting beside Leticia was no doubt the reason. Her hand lay on the velvet between them. He reached for it but hesitated when he heard a tap at the door.

Mary entered with the port in a crystal decanter and two glasses. The tray held a teapot covered with a cozy, toast wrapped in a white napkin, and jam in a little glass dish. She set it on the table in front of Leticia.

"Thank you, Mary. You may go home now. I will not need you until morning."

"But, ma'am, I . . ."

"Good night," insisted Leticia. She poured some port into the glasses.

The thought flashed through Nat's mind that he would be compromising Leticia by being alone in the house with her, but she did not seem to mind. Handing him a glass, she leaned back into the corner of the sofa and watched him through half-closed eyes.

He swallowed the ruby liquid and found it warmed his insides all the way down. He sat silently for a few minutes, letting the fire and port relax him. He'd eaten nothing since midday, and the drink went straight to his head. The toast—maybe that would help. He reached for it, only to watch it slip from the napkin to the floor.

Leticia knelt down in front of him to pick up the toast. He stretched his hand out and touched a ringlet of her hair, letting it wind around his finger. It felt like the silky strands of floss his mother used to embroider.

Leticia was still for a moment, then in a soft voice said, "You had better remove your boots; they are very wet." She put her hand upon his knee as if for support as she rose.

"Your breeches are soaked!" she exclaimed. "We must get you into something dry before you catch the ague."

She led him into her dressing room and handed him a man's

silk robe. "Put this on. I am sure you'll be more comfortable out of those wet clothes." She brushed against him and left him alone to undress. The warmth of her body heightened his senses.

When he walked into the boudoir, she was waiting for him. She drew him into an embrace and lifted her lips for his kiss. Her breath fluttered over his cheek, and the fragrance of violets tantalized his nose. She whispered, "This is for that bruise on your chin."

The feel of her lips on his was sweet. She led him to the sofa, where he leaned back against the soft pillows. Warmed by the fire, he relaxed until his eyes grew heavy, and he fell asleep.

"Sleep on, Mr. B. You really are just a boy." Leticia shrugged and entered her bedroom.

Chapter Eleven

Nat awoke with a splitting headache and a mouth as dry as cotton. The fragrance of violets filled his senses and brought back memories of a kiss the night before. He opened his eyes to find he was curled up on the sofa in Leticia's boudoir. He felt his face flush with embarrassment. His conscience told him Deverell had been right. The mixture of alcohol and an experienced woman had been more than he could handle. Funny, he couldn't remember a thing after Leticia kissed him.

In his haste to sit up, he knocked the candle off its holder onto the table. He tiptoed into the dressing room and peeked into the bedroom. Leticia lay with her back to him. Her blond curls spilled over the pillow. She was asleep. Good. He shut the door and threw the robe onto the chair. His breeches, damp and wrinkled, chilled his legs as he pulled them on and tucked in his shirt.

Coat and boots lay by the fireplace in the boudoir. He pushed his feet into his boots and slid his arms into the riding coat still moist from the rain. He tucked his cravat into a pocket. The handkerchief fell to the floor, but he failed to notice.

He ran quietly down the stairs. The housekeeper would be arriving soon. At the front door he peered out and hurried down the street to the livery. Waking the hostler, he asked for the nearest hotel. Nat grabbed his valise from the storage cupboard and walked to the place a block away.

His insistent ringing of the bell brought the owner of the hotel out from a room behind the desk. His hair standing up on the back of his head, the sleepy man rubbed his eyes.

" 'Ow can I 'elp you, sir?"

"A room and some hot water. I'll want breakfast in about an hour."

"Yes, sir, I'll take care of it. I'll show you to your room now." He climbed the stairs. Nat followed close behind. "The 'ot water will be up in a few minutes, sir," the man said as he lit the lamp and left the room.

Nat unpacked his clothes and laid them on the bed. The place was clean enough, though not first-rate. When the hot water arrived, he undressed, glad to be rid of his damp clothes. After a wash, he brushed his hair and sat down on the lumpy mattress, sighing deeply. Shoulders slumped, hands on his knees, he tried to remember what had happened. His mother would be disappointed if she knew he'd stayed in Leticia's house last night. Perhaps she'd never find out. Even his father, who was more inclined to think "boys will be boys," would be disappointed.

He'd talk to the men whose names his father had given him, and then he'd go home. The city wasn't the place for him.

There was a knock at the door, and a voice said, "Breakfast, sir."

He opened the door to a middle-aged woman, her gray hair drawn back tightly in a small bun at the nape of her neck. She had a long face and sallow skin, but her smile was broad and her voice pleasant.

"Ye didn't say what ye wanted, so I've brought a little bit of everything—a rasher of bacon, a sausage or two, tatties, and some bread." She brought in the tray with the food and a pot of tea and set it on the small table by the bed. "There now, will ye be wanting anything else, sir?" She bobbed her head as she stood in the doorway.

"No, thank you," Nat said, for if the truth were told, food turned his stomach at the moment. He sat down on the bed and took a bite of potato and then some sausage. He was hungry after all. When he finished, he put on a clean cravat and a coat. He'd call on the men his father had suggested. One of them might have a place for him in their business.

* * *

The rider watched the first rays of sun break through, painting the clouds deep shades of pink and red with gold around the edges. More rain, he thought; a good day for staying indoors. He gave a deep-throated chuckle.

Only a few more blocks to Leticia's. He should make the vixen wait longer, but he couldn't stop thinking about her. Even though when he was with her she drove him to distraction, he had to have her. This gift would seal the bargain. He was eager to see her, although it was early.

The flower market was coming alive, and he looked for his favorite flower seller.

"'Ello, sir," she said as she recognized him. "And is it the violets fer ye this early morning?"

"No, roses, red ones."

"I 'ave some beauties, I 'ave. Look at these, sir," she said. She picked out a dozen and tied the stems together with a string.

"They will do nicely." He put some coins into her hand and watched her eyes light up.

"Thank ye kindly, sir." She gave him a bright smile.

The man unlocked the door and climbed the back stairs to Leticia's. He laid the flowers on the chest and peeked in the bedroom door. He smiled at her sleeping form. In the dressing room he found the silk lounging robe on the chair, the sash on the floor. He picked up the sash and held it in his hands. What was this doing here? He dropped it onto the chair. Removing his coat and jacket, he slipped his arms into the robe, tied the fringed sash around his waist, and put a small box into his pocket. In the bedroom, he leaned over and kissed her bare shoulder, murmuring her name.

She sighed and whispered, "Awake at last, you lazy boy?"

Ripping the sheet back, he exclaimed, "What do you mean, 'awake at last'?"

Her eyes flew open. She glanced at the empty bed beside her and pulled the sheet up to cover herself. "Darling! You frightened me."

"You didn't sound frightened to me."

"Don't be silly. I was dreaming, that's all. I've missed you. Have you missed me?" she said. "Did you come to say you are sorry for neglecting me?"

He took a shuddering breath and said, "I've missed you terribly. I brought you something to show you how much." He reached into his pocket and drew out the box.

She caressed his hand as she took it. Her eyes grew large, for lying on the velvet was the most exquisite sapphire bracelet.

"Oh, it's lovely. Please put it on for me."

He sat down beside her and clasped the expensive bauble onto her arm, kissing the inside of her wrist.

"The gems reminded me of the color of your eyes."

He pulled her close, covering her warm lips with his eager, demanding ones.

"I brought you roses too," he murmured.

"Bring them to me," she whispered.

He reluctantly let go of her and entered the boudoir. Reaching for the roses, he noticed two glasses on the table and the candle knocked from its holder. Someone had been drinking port. Under the sofa a piece of white caught his eye. He picked it up and smoothed it out. Fine stitches sewn in blue thread made the monogram NB. He cursed under his breath.

His fingers clenched around the handkerchief; then he threw it to the floor and mashed it beneath his heel. *How could she, the trollop? She won't make a mockery of me.* He clenched his jaw while rocking back and forth on the balls of his feet. He picked up the roses and walked back into the bedroom.

He laid the flowers on her dresser and said, "I thought you'd enjoy these."

"They're lovely. I must put them in water."

"Do that later, my dear. Turn over and let me rub your back for you."

With a sigh, she turned over. Untying the sash from his waist, he sat on the side of the bed. The fringe on the sash tickled her back as he dangled it over her. She laughed. His jaw clenched, and his eyes narrowed. He leaned over her and slipped the sash around her neck. Her laugh, like light silver bells, ended with an outcry and gasp as he tightened it. She clawed at the fabric, desperate sounds emanating from her throat, then silence. Even when he felt her body relax, he continued to hold the sash tightly. At last his fingers loosened. He rose and took the sash from her neck and the bracelet from her wrist. The exertion had raised perspiration on his brow, but his body felt clammy, and his breath came in short bursts.

He dressed, folded the robe, and returned it to the dressing room. Putting the bracelet back into the box, he slipped it into the pocket of his coat. He took the roses from the dresser and left the handkerchief on the floor.

He had to leave before the housekeeper arrived. He made his way down the back stairs and threw the flowers into the dustbin. No one knew he was here. He'd never be suspected. He mounted his horse and rode out.

Intent on the street ahead of him, the gentleman didn't see the costermonger trundling his cart of vegetables. The produce vendor stopped to catch his breath on the way to the marketplace. He saw the man come out the door at the side of the house, get on a fine black horse, and ride in the opposite direction.

"Somethin' havey-cavey going on here," the costermonger murmured to himself. "What's a swell of the first stare doin' in this neighborhood? O' course, he might 'ave been visiting his ladylove."

Nat, tired and hungry, returned to the hotel at dinnertime. Not one of the places he'd visited appealed to him. There must be something he could do that he'd enjoy.

Nat stopped at the desk. "Wake me at seven thirty. I'll be leaving after breakfast."

He found a quiet corner in the dining room and ate the mutton and potatoes smothered in a thin gravy. Maybe tomorrow would be a better day if his conscience would ease a bit.

* * *

The morning sky lightened through a misty swirl of fog. Nat awakened from a sleep haunted by dreams to a knock on his door.

"It is seven thirty, sir. I have hot water for ye."

Nat, tangled in his blankets from a restless night, called out, "Bring it in."

After a hasty toilette, Nat dressed, packed his clothes, and bounded down the stairs, eager for breakfast. He called to the young girl waiting on the tables and gave her his breakfast order. Once finished, he strolled outside, keen to see what the day was like. Disappointed by the swirling, dirty mist, he couldn't wait to leave this foggy, miserable town.

A small boy in a cap and knee pants materialized out of the haze, carrying newspapers under his arm and shouting, "Woman found dead in Newbury Court. Police suspect foul play. Wan' a paper, mister?"

Nat handed the boy a coin and took the paper. He read the headline, then, with horror, read on.

YOUNG BEAUTY FOUND DEAD

Leticia Browning was found murdered in her bed by her housekeeper, Mary Smith, when Miss Smith came to work yesterday morning. Police say Smith saw a man at the house the night before the murder. They would not reveal the way in which Miss Browning was killed or if they had any other clues. They are searching the area for anyone else who might have seen the man. The housekeeper gave a description of him: young, medium height, brown hair and eyes. They hope to have a sketch of the suspect soon to help in his apprehension.

Nat leaned against the wall of a building for support as he finished reading the article, his heart pounding in his ears. He couldn't believe what he'd read. Why would someone want to kill her?

He reread the last few lines. It was a description of him, but

Leticia was alive when he left. It must have happened soon after. Was the murderer in the house when he was there? The thought sent prickles along his skin.

He thought he could leave this escapade behind, but now it had come back to haunt him.

Folding the paper and putting it under his arm, he ran up the stairs to the room and picked up his valise. Perspiration sprinkled his upper lip and dampened his armpits.

His meal was ready when he returned to the dining room. His stomach rebelled at the thought of food, but he knew he must eat, and he needed time to think. Breakfast eaten, he paid his tab and set out for the stable. Around the corner he saw the hostler talking to two men. One was a constable, and the other must be a Bow Street Runner. The liveryman waved his hands and pointed in his direction just as Nat stepped back into the secluded doorway of the building on the corner.

His chest constricted, and a cold sweat broke out on his forehead. The filly was lost to him. He'd be lucky to escape with the Runners searching for him. He waited in the shadows as the two men strode by, then eased his way out and scanned the area for the hostler. The man had gone inside the stable. Across the street and down an alleyway Nat dashed. To put as much distance between himself and the law was all he could think of as he disappeared into the fog.

The butler knocked on Stanhope's bedroom door, then entered. "There's a constable downstairs asking for you, Master Fielding. He's quite insistent he see you immediately."

"Tell him I'll be down in a half hour, and send up a pot of tea, Benham."

Stanhope entered the small study forty-five minutes later.

"How may I help you?" he asked the man.

Dwarfed by the large chair, the man rose with his hat in his gnarled hands. "Constable Billings is the name, sir. I received a packet this morning from the magistrate at Bow Street. He asked me to give you some news that you may find disturbing." The man's firm voice belied his frail look.

"Well, out with it, man."

"Miss Leticia Browning was found murdered in her home day before yesterday. The housekeeper, Mary Smith, said you paid the rent on the establishment and were very close to Miss Browning."

Stanhope's mouth dropped open. The news took his breath away. For a moment the room swirled before his eyes.

The constable saw his face turn white. "You'd better sit down, sir." He reached for a nearby chair and pushed it behind Stanhope.

"I can't believe it. She was here . . . a few days ago. Who did this vile thing?"

"Don't know yet, sir, but there was a clue or two left behind. Do you know anyone who calls himself Mr. B?"

Stanhope shook his head.

"What about someone with the initials *NB*?"

Stanhope hesitated. "I, ah, well, there is someone, but it couldn't be he. No, I am sure it's not he." *Not Deverell's brother, Nat.*

"If you know anything, sir, you must tell me." Constable Billings set his hat on a table and took a pad of paper and a small pencil from his pocket.

"There's a young man who lives nearby whose name's Nathaniel Bromfield. I have known the family for years." *Nat was infatuated with Leticia. But, no, it couldn't be Nat.*

"When was the last time you saw him?"

Stanhope took the decanter of brandy off the table. He poured himself a drink with a trembling hand. He must get control of his thoughts. "Last week, here in my home. I was having a party."

"Was Miss Browning here also?" The little man continued to probe.

Stanhope sighed. "She was." He took a large swallow of the brandy.

"And . . ." The constable stood and took a couple of steps closer to Stanhope.

Stanhope ran his fingers through his hair. "Well, they danced once, I think."

"Anything else happen?" He cocked his head and leaned in closer.

"Just a little thing—'twas really not important. Nat had a fight with one of the guests, and then he went home."

"What was the fight about?"

"I really don't know; you will have to ask the men involved."

"What was the name of the other man?"

Stanhope stood up. "Lord Brendan Helmsley."

The constable moved back. "One more question, sir. Where were you last Monday night and Tuesday morning?"

Stanhope's eyes hardened. "If that is all, I would like to be alone. I shall send my butler down with the addresses for Bromfield and Helmsley and where I was as well." Stanhope turned on his heel and left the room. *Why, my beautiful Leticia, why?*

The constable bit his lip. Was Mr. Stanhope hiding something?

He waited until the butler brought him the addresses and stuffed the paper into his pocket. He retrieved his hat and followed the man to the back door.

The Bromfields lived close by. He'd visit them as well. He rummaged through his grimy leather saddlebag until he found the envelope containing the monogrammed handkerchief.

"We shall see what you have to say for yourself, Mr. Bromfield," he murmured as he mounted his horse, and he gave the reins a flick.

"I expect Nat will be home today." Anne Louise and her husband had just returned from the home of her sister.

Fredrick handed his coat and hat to the parlor maid. "I hope he's here before dinner. I'm anxious to hear how he fared with those interviews, and I'll be leaving for London tomorrow early. Wonder how Deverell did at the factory this week."

She rang for the maid. "Nelly, bring us some tea and biscuits in the sitting room. Will that keep you until luncheon, Mr. Bromfield?"

"Very well, my dear."

She had poured her husband a cup of tea when the butler came into the sitting room.

"There's a man, a constable, in the hall, sir, who would like to see Master Nathaniel. I told him he's not at home, but he insists on seeing you and Mrs. Bromfield."

"Show him in, Williams."

"Whatever would a constable want with Nat?" Anne Louise said. Her brow puckered in a frown.

"I cannot imagine, my dear," her husband replied. "We'll know soon enough."

Mr. Bromfield stood when the constable entered the room. "Would you like to join us in a cup of tea and some biscuits, sir?" He motioned the man to a chair.

"Thank you, a cuppa would be nice. My name is Billings, Constable Billings. Sorry to barge in on you like this, but I've important business with Nathaniel Bromfield. I understand he's not at home."

Mr. Bromfield sat on the edge of his chair. "He's been in London for a few days, but we expect him home tonight. Can we help you in any way?"

"When did your son go to London?" The man addressed Mr. Bromfield.

"He left in the early afternoon on Monday. What is this about, sir?" Agitation showed on Fredrick's face.

"A friend of his was murdered on Tuesday morning."

Anne Louise gasped. "Who?"

"Murdered? Good grief, man, who was it?" Mr. Bromfield leaned over to take his wife's hand.

"It was a woman, sir, a Miss Leticia Browning."

"Never heard Nat mention anyone by that name. Have you, Mrs. Bromfield?"

"No, at least I don't think so. I heard the boys talking about some friend of Stanhope's, but I do not remember a name."

" 'Boys,' ma'am?" The constable gazed at Mrs. Bromfield.

"Nathaniel and his older brother, Deverell." She clasped her husband's hand with both of hers.

"And when was this, ma'am?" The constable's voice was placid and unhurried.

"A . . . a few days before Nat went to London."

"Well, I thank you kindly for your time and the tea," Constable Billings said as he rose from his chair. He set the teacup on the table in front of Mrs. Bromfield and asked her one more question. "Would you recognize this?" He drew the monogrammed handkerchief from his coat pocket and handed it to her.

"Why, yes. I embroidered this for Nathaniel's last birthday. But where did you get it?" she asked as her cheeks paled and her heart quickened.

"I really can't tell you any more, but I'm sure we'll be talking again." He took the handkerchief from her hand and swiftly left the room.

Constable Billings mounted his old mare and looked back at the house. One of his men would watch the house tonight. He must catch the boy if he returned home. The magistrate would want to interrogate Mr. Nathaniel Bromfield. Too bad; his parents seemed like nice people.

Chapter Twelve

Deverell's high-collared shirt and gold double-breasted waistcoat were still tidy, although he'd loosened his cravat and noticed that the edges of his cuffs were dirty. He'd spent the whole morning with the bookkeeper. The knock on the door was a welcome relief from all the figures swirling before his eyes.

The clerk stuck his head in to say, "There's a Mr. Lucian Moreton to see you, sir."

"Show him in, Edgar." Deverell stood to welcome his friend. "Good to see you, Moreton."

"Have you seen Stanhope?" Lucian's voice sounded anxious.

The two men stood in front of Deverell's desk. Lucian's eyes were puffy and red-rimmed. From lack of sleep or drinking, Deverell couldn't tell. "What's wrong, man? You look terrible."

"Leticia Browning is dead."

Deverell's eyes widened. "Dead? I saw her a few days ago, and she was fine."

The creases deepened over Lucian's nose. "She was murdered."

Deverell sank onto the edge of his desk. "Murdered! Good grief, man. I can't believe it. Who would do such a thing?"

Lucian took the newspaper from under his arm. "It's all in here."

Deverell skimmed the front page, then laid it beside him. "Why would anyone want to kill Leticia?"

"It seems the police have a description of her last visitor. Some clues were left, but they are not giving out much information." Lucian twisted the ring on his little finger.

Deverell ran his hand through his hair. "I'll go see Stanhope as soon as I'm home. He may know more."

"Thought you'd like to know. I don't mind telling you, it was a shock. I still can't believe it myself. I'd like to stay and talk, but I have another appointment. Let me know how Stanhope is. Tell him I'll see him as soon as I can." Lucian left and closed the door behind him.

Deverell picked up the newspaper as he eased himself into the chair.

Leticia Browning was found dead in her bed by her housekeeper Mary Smith. . . . When he saw the description of the suspect, he gasped and read it again.

That sounded a great deal like his brother, but it could also describe a great many other men. He wondered if this was why Lucian had brought him the paper. Whatever the housekeeper said, his brother didn't kill Leticia. Father would be here tomorrow morning. He could tell him if Nat had been in London.

Fredrick Bromfield entered Deverell's office at the mill the next morning with a worried look on his face. "Have you seen Nathaniel?" he demanded of his older son.

"He's in London?" Deverell frowned. "Father, have you heard?"

"About Leticia Browning? Yesterday we had a visit from a Constable Billings. Since then I've read the story in the newspaper. I thought Nathaniel would explain why he was at Miss Browning's house when he came in last night, but he didn't come home. I'm afraid he's in the devil's own scrape—he's their primary suspect. Of all the half-witted things to do. Why was he at the woman's house?" His voice was edged with anger and his face dangerously flushed.

"Sit down, Father." Deverell led him to a chair, then leaned against the desk. "Are you sure Nat was there?"

"This Constable Billings had a handkerchief your mother had monogrammed for Nat's birthday. I am sure it was found in her house. How else could the police have it?"

"Maybe it was stolen?" Deverell offered with little enthusiasm.

His father gave him a hopeful look; then his face fell. "He was there, wasn't he?"

Deverell hesitated. "He was dangling after the girl the night of the party. He came to fisticuffs with Lord Helmsley over a remark the man made about her. Nat had had some wine, and you know he can't hold his liquor."

"Who is this woman?" His father's face showed his confusion.

"She was Stanhope's mistress. He paid the rent on her house and had furnished it for her."

"Dash it, boy, why did you let your brother chase after this light skirt?"

"I tried to tell him he was making a gudgeon of himself, but he wouldn't listen. He flew up in the boughs when I told him what she was. I went to Stanhope's party that night to keep an eye on him."

Fredrick Bromfield reached out and clasped his son's knee. "I'm sorry, Deverell. I should have known that. Nat can be hotheaded, but I can't see him hurting a woman, much less murder." He rubbed his jaw with the palm of his hand.

"None of this makes sense, but I'm going to get to the bottom of it," said Deverell. "I'll start with the housekeeper. She may still be at Leticia's."

His father gave him a questioning look. "Do you know where Miss Browning lived?"

"I was there once before Leticia moved in." Deverell opened up the books lying on the desk. "If you'd like, I'll show you what has occurred at the factory this week; then I can go look for the housekeeper."

"Yes, yes. Let's get to it." Fredrick sat in the chair behind the desk.

The housekeeper wasn't at Leticia's that afternoon, but Deverell found the livery where Nat had left his horse. Inside, the hostler was currying a gray stallion.

"I sent 'im to the 'otel down the street early the next mornin'," said the man. "A sweet goer, his 'orse is. She's still 'ere, ya know. I don't suppose ya'd like to pay the bill?"

"I'll pay you for the days she's been here," said Deverell as he reached into a small leather purse.

"Thank ya kindly," said the man, and he held out his dirt-creased hand for the coins.

"Would you saddle her for me while I talk to the manager at the hotel?"

"Of course, guv'ner. It's right around that corner," he said, pointing to the right.

The owner of the hotel told Deverell, "'E came in early of a mornin' lookin' like 'e'd been dippin' rather deep. Asked for a room, a bath, and breakfast. 'E had supper and slept 'ere that night too. The next mornin' 'e was down early for 'is breakfast. Nellie took 'is order. I'll call 'er."

"Thank you."

A young girl of fifteen or so in a simple dress and apron came to the front desk.

"Miss, I'd like to ask you about a young man who stayed here a few days ago," Deverell said.

"The one the Bow Street Runner's been askin' about?" When Deverell nodded, she continued. "He went out to get a paper while he was waitin' fer 'is breakfast. When he came back in, he got his bag and sat at that table right there." She pointed toward the back of the room. "I remember he looked kinda worrit. Then he had his breakfast and left."

"Thank you, miss." Deverell turned back to the hotel owner. "Did you get his name?"

"If they pay cash up front, I don't take no names. We get a lot of men who only stay for a few hours, and they don't like leavin' a name, if ye get my drift. When the Runners came, I told them just what I'm tellin' ye."

"I see. Well, thanks. By the way, do you remember what he was wearing when he left?" Deverell tried one more time for some clue he could follow.

"'E had on tan ridin' breeches and black boots. I don't remember the color of his coat or if he had a 'at on. 'E was young, probably 'ere to sow a few wild oats. Looks like 'e got 'imself in the suds."

Deverell thanked the man again and went outside. He mustn't let apprehension overtake him. He'd stay focused on finding Nat.

Which way would he have gone? The principal officers were at the livery to his right. He wouldn't go that way. There'd been a dreadful London fog that day, the hostler had said. It would have been easy for Nat to lose himself in that haze. There was a small alleyway down by the corner. Would he have taken that and stayed off the main roads?

Walking across the street, Deverell mounted his horse and led Nat's back to the stables at the mill. The alley was where he'd start looking after he talked to Leticia's housekeeper.

At the Bow Street station Saturday morning Stanhope asked if there'd been any break in the murder investigation of Leticia Browning.

The constable at the front desk said, "The Runners are on the job, but they ain't found the young man yet. You know we only have part of his name and the description the housekeeper gave us to go on. No one else saw or heard anything amiss at the house. We did have a picture drawn and took it around the neighborhood. The hostler at a nearby stable had seen him, but he didn't know his name. The man at the hotel warn't no help either. Fellow just disappeared into the fog, so they say. We're still working on it, sir."

Stanhope found it hard to a keep a civil tongue. They couldn't find one callow youth. The boy knew little of London and should have been found long before this. If Sir John Fielding were still magistrate, they would have caught him by now.

"Give me a copy of the sketch you have of the man." Stanhope couldn't keep the disgust out of his voice. He snatched the paper from the man and stuffed it into his pocket.

Outside, he mounted his horse and sat hunched over in the saddle, his head down as he rode toward Mary Smith's home.

She could pack up Leticia's things on Monday. Tuesday, he'd tell the landlord he was free to rent the house at the end of the quarter.

A loud voice yelled, "Look where you're going, fool!"

Stanhope's horse reared and almost unseated him as a carriage came bowling down the street, missing him by inches.

He spoke soothingly to his horse, pulling the reins in tightly as it sidestepped, its eyes wide and nostrils flared. Hands shaking, Stanhope proceeded through the crowded streets. Guiding the horse into a narrow alleyway, he dismounted and knocked on the door of a small, shabby house whose yard was swept clean.

Mary Smith opened the door. "Oh, Mr. Stanhope," she said, her lips quivering, "I'm so sorry." She couldn't say more.

His mouth twisted in a grimace. "We will catch the blighter, Mary."

"Oh, yes, sir, I surely 'ope so."

"I'd like you to pack Miss Leticia's things on Monday, please. I'll be closing the house at the end of the week."

"Wh . . . Where shall I send them?"

"I'll have a carter pick them up on Friday." He handed her an envelope. "I've given you an extra month's pay and a letter of reference to help you find another job."

"Thank you, sir." Her nose reddened, and she was clearly about to burst into tears.

Stanhope couldn't watch her cry. "Good-bye, Mary." He turned abruptly to his mount.

Looking for a place to escape for a few hours, he dropped into his favorite gambling establishment. After a hand of faro he wandered around the room, speaking occasionally to an acquaintance. A familiar, dejected-looking face caught his gaze.

Stanhope leaned over and remarked to his friend, "Lost at cards again, I see."

Smiling a bit grimly, Lucian Moreton stood up. "Good to see you, Stanhope. I say, I am surprised to see you in town since Miss Browning . . . well, you know."

"Actually, I am in town on that matter. Have you had dinner

yet? No? Let us find a place we can eat and talk. I need to get out of the crush." He had decided what he needed to do.

They found a well-kept parlor in a tavern nearby and ordered a dinner of roast beef and a bottle of claret. When the wine was served, Stanhope said, "There's someone I'm trying to find. I wonder if you would be free to help me. I'd pay you, of course, and all your expenses. Are you interested?" Lucian's gambling habit generally kept him with pockets to let.

"What did you have in mind?" Lucian asked. "Who are you looking for?"

"This man." Stanhope held out the picture. His hand trembled as he held out the paper.

"Nat Bromfield?" Lucian's eyes widened in surprise. "Is this the man Bow Street suspects of the murder?"

Stanhope stiffened. "He's the man." The muscles in his jaw were so tight, they hurt.

"But why are you looking for him?"

"The Runners are doing nothing," Stanhope replied through clenched teeth.

"I see," Lucian replied. "What makes you think I can find him when they have failed?" He played with the ring on his little finger, a look of uncertainty in his eyes.

"Because I will pay you for as long as it takes, and there will be an extra five hundred pounds when you find him and he is brought to trial."

"You are most generous, and you are right: I have been drawing the bustle too freely at the gaming tables."

"I want him brought to justice."

"You've done me more than one favor in the past. I can certainly repay you with a few weeks of my time," said Lucian.

The two men looked up as Lord Brendan Helmsley spoke to them. "Mind if I join you, gentlemen?" He sat down without waiting for an answer.

"Would like to apologize for the situation at your party the other night, Stanhope, but the boy brought me to a point non plus, and I could not ignore him. Of course, in light of all that has happened since, I wish I had. He told me when he came outside that he intended to have Miss Browning one way or the other. I am sorry, Stanhope. Lucky the police found that monogrammed handkerchief."

Stanhope bowed his head in acknowledgment.

"Well, I must return to my friends." Lord Helmsley stood and sauntered off.

When he was out of earshot, Lucian leaned across the table. "Helmsley has a reputation for using his fists at the drop of a hat. I've heard he's beaten up his fancy women as well—deadly jealous, they say." He scowled. "Do you think Bromfield really said that?"

"I don't know. He might have if provoked enough," Stanhope answered.

"If he didn't, why would Helmsley lie?"

Stanhope shrugged. He was convinced of Nat's guilt.

Chapter Thirteen

A tear coursed down Mary's cheek as she swept off the stoop at the house on Newbury Court early Monday morning. Miss Leticia had been difficult at times, but she would miss her. The housekeeper sighed, brushed the tears away, and turned to go into the house, when a stranger rode up. The young man dismounted and walked over to her, a disarming smile on his face.

"Are you Mary Smith?" the gentleman asked.

"Yes, sir."

"I am Deverell Bromfield, a friend of Fielding Stanhope's, and I'd like to ask some questions, if you don't mind."

"'E never mentioned you when I saw 'im."

"I'm trying to help solve this terrible crime. I'm sure you are interested in seeing justice done."

"I'd like to see the blighter 'ung, sir."

Deverell winced. "May I come in?" he asked.

"Of course," Mary said as she opened the door. "Would you mind coming to the kitchen, sir?"

He followed her through the dark hall and down a few steps. On the nearby stove sat a kettle, steam rising from its spout. A bench and wooden chair were arranged in front of the fireplace. She motioned him to the chair.

"Some tea, sir? I have the pot on."

"No, thank you. Do you mind if I call you Mary?"

She gave him a brief shake of her head.

"Now, Mary, would you mind repeating everything you told the magistrate?" He sat in the chair and motioned for her to sit on the bench.

Reluctantly, she sat on the edge of it and twisted her hands in her lap. Her description of the man at Leticia's tallied with the one in the newspaper.

"The mistress invited 'im up to 'er boudoir. I brought some toast, jam, a pot of tea, and a decanter of port up to the room before I went 'ome for the night."

Deverell leaned forward, giving her his full attention. "Tell me exactly what you found when you came in the next morning."

"I came in the back door, like I always do." She picked at a loose thread on her apron.

"Was it locked?" he asked.

She sat up straight. "Yes, sir."

"Then what?" His voice was crisp.

"There was no sound, so I knew Miss Leticia wasn't up yet. I went into the kitchen and stirred the banked fire in the stove and put the teakettle on. The mistress liked tea and toast when she woke up. About nine, I took the tea and toast upstairs. The door to the boudoir was open, and I put the tray on the table. I went to the bedroom and knocked. There was no answer, so I peeked in the door. The mistress was sprawled across the bed all funny-like. When I touched 'er shoulder, it was cold, and I could see 'er face. It was terrible. Her eyes were . . ." She put her hand to her mouth to cover a sob.

Deverell reached over and patted her shoulder. "Maybe we should have that tea now," he said.

Mary took a hanky from her apron pocket and wiped her eyes as she stood. "Yes, sir, I'll get it for you."

She took the hot kettle from the stove and poured the water into the pot, letting it steep a few minutes. She set the pot and cups on a tray and brought it to the bench. Mary poured them both a cup and handed one to Deverell.

He took the tea. "What did you do next?"

"I ran downstairs and sent one of the boys on the street to get a watchman. When the man came, I sent him upstairs, and I stayed in the kitchen until the magistrate and a constable came." She blew her nose, then twisted the hanky in her hands.

Deverell waited a moment before he continued. "Can you

answer another question?" At her nod he asked, "Did you find or see anything in the next few days that was out of the ordinary or unusual?"

"The constable wouldn't let me back in the 'ouse until the next day. I guess they were investigating. I cleaned up the downstairs, as I still couldn't bring myself to go into her room. I took a pan out to the dustbin to empty it, and I saw something strange there—a bouquet of red roses 'ung up on something at the top. They were not there the night before she died, and that Mr. B 'adn't brought them with 'im."

Deverell stood up, urgency overtaking him. "Where is the dustbin?"

She set down her cup, and he followed her into a back hall.

She pointed. "It's right there by the back door before you go up the stairs."

He lifted the door and saw a piece of raised metal where the nail had worked loose.

"Mr. Stanhope had it put in the wall so I could put the dirt into it from the inside. That's where I found the roses. They were stuck on that piece of metal at the top."

"You said you came in the back door the morning you found Leticia, and the door was locked?"

"Yes, sir." She nodded her head.

"You have told no one else about the roses?"

"No, sir. Is it important?" Her heart lifted with hope that the killer might be found.

"It may be." He walked back into the kitchen and sat down. "Mary, you must be entirely honest with me."

She gave him a wary look from where she stood behind the bench.

"Did any other man besides Stanhope visit her?"

Unwilling to besmirch the name of her mistress, she hesitated.

"Please, Mary, I need to know."

"One or two," she reluctantly admitted.

"What were their names?"

Her hand on her hip, she said, "Miss Leticia only saw them

on my day off, and she never told me who they were. She made me promise never to tell Mr. Stanhope. She said they were friends o' 'ers and she had a right to have friends over."

"I'm sure she thought so. One other question. Was the front door locked that morning?"

She closed her eyes and pursed her lips. "I opened it for the watchman, and it was . . . unlocked. I locked it the night before. I know I did."

"Thank you for your help, and here's something for your trouble. I'll show myself out."

Deverell's mouth turned up slightly at the corners. Someone had brought Leticia roses and then thrown them away. That person had a key to the back door. If the front door was open, it was likely Nat had left that way. At last he had some evidence that someone else had been there. A ray of hope lightened the load he had been carrying. He turned his head from side to side and stretched to loosen the muscles in his neck and back before he mounted Queen Bess.

He would find the murderer. His heart constricted at the thought of his brother being hanged. That would not happen. He'd see that it didn't. He needed to find the flower seller, but first he wanted to see Alexi. He wanted to tell her personally about Nat and explain that his brother could not have murdered the woman. He rode the mare at a casual pace through the streets as he went over in his mind everything Mary Smith had told him.

Mr. Bromfield was waiting in his office. "What is the news, son?"

Deverell hung his coat on a hook and placed his topper on the shelf above. He drew a chair up to his father's desk and related his conversation with Leticia Browning's housekeeper. "I'll try to find the flower seller this afternoon. But I'd like to go home briefly before I start my search for Nat."

Deverell hugged his mother while she cried into his jacket. His own eyes were moist and his throat tight. "Father sends his love, and I wanted to see you before I leave to find Nathaniel."

She smiled at him through her tears. "I know you will find him."

Her hand in the crook of his arm, she led him to the parlor. "Dinner will be ready soon. I am sure you are hungry after your ride from London."

He stood by the sofa as his mother took a seat. "After dinner I'll ride over and see the Moretons. I would like to tell Alexi and her family what is going on." His cheeks flushed as he saw his mother's smile at the use of Alexandra's nickname.

"Do you have feelings for Alexandra?"

"I admire her a great deal. And it would be a shock to our friends to read about Nat in the news. Someone from the family should tell them. That's why I am going there tonight. If you don't mind, I'll go upstairs and bathe and change for dinner." He squeezed his mother's hand before he left the room.

A few clouds scudded through the evening sky, but the stars winked between them. The lively breeze on Deverell's face induced him to give his topper a firm pat. The leaves wove patterns of light and dark on the road as the moon contended with the clouds. It was a pleasant evening in spite of the gentle wind, and he was eager to see Alexi.

The lights shone in the parlor window as Deverell handed his horse over to the groom. His hands were clammy and his throat dry. How did he tell someone that his own brother was suspected of murder? He'd have to tell Alexi straight out. He didn't know of any other way.

"I'd like to speak to Miss Moreton, please," he told the maid who answered the door.

"I shall see if she is available, sir."

On her way to the front hall, Isabel heard voices. "Deverell, how nice to see you. What brings you here this evening?"

"I'd like to speak with your daughter, if that is possible."

"Of course. Alexandra is in the parlor. Go right in." She followed him in, then busied herself with her embroidery on the other side of the room.

Alexi sat on the settee, a book in her hand. Her eyes lit up as he entered the room.

"Alexi, I hope I am not interrupting your evening."

She stood and returned his bow with a curtsy. "It is nice to see you. Come sit down, please. You look so solemn. Is a member of your family ill?"

"Something has happened that has caused my family a great deal of grief. I didn't want you to hear it from another source." His voice was low.

She looked at him with eyes full of compassion and reached out her hand to him.

"My brother, Nathaniel, has been accused of murdering a young woman."

Her mother looked up as Alexi gasped.

"I know my brother, and he is not capable of such a deed, no matter what the evidence says to the contrary. I have been investigating on my own and found some clues. The boy ran when he knew he was suspected. I leave soon to find him, and I don't know how long I shall be gone."

"Deverell, I hardly know what to say. I can't imagine Nathaniel murdering anyone. Your parents must be overwhelmed. What can I do to help?"

Deverell's heart felt lighter at her response. "Tell them what you just told me. That will encourage them, I know."

"My mother and I will visit them tomorrow and assure them of our concern. I shall be praying that you find Nat safe and that you'll soon prove his innocence."

His heart filled with gratitude and warmth, he said, "You are a true friend, Alexi. I'll call on you again as soon as I'm home." He turned her hand over and touched his lips to her palm. "Good night, my dear friend."

Alexi closed her fingers over the warmth of his kiss on her hand.

Chapter Fourteen

Nat huddled in the doorway of a shop. It was the only place he had found to sleep that night. The door opened, and a cloud of dust and dirt covered him.

"Hey, what's this? *Achoo!* Didn't you see me here?" he complained. Another sneeze rent the air. He looked up at the young boy who stood above him with a broom in his hand.

The lad chuckled. "Don't ya know better than to be sleepin' in a doorway this time o' mornin? Ye're lucky it was only a bit of dust and not a swift kick to the backside."

Nat stood up, furious with himself for being caught in such a ridiculous position. He continued to shake the dust off his clothes. "I'm sorry I haven't learned all the rules of the street yet." He ran his hand through his curly brown hair, sending specks of dust into the air.

"Not long on yer own, huh?" the boy asked. His face still wore an amused look.

"Long enough," was the disgruntled reply.

"My name is Henry," the young boy said, holding out his hand.

"I am Nat . . . Nathan . . . Broome," he improvised, then took the extended hand and gave it a shake.

"Ye're new round here. Lookin' fer work?"

"Well, yes, I am. Don't happen to know of something, do you?"

"Maybe," he said, "but you'd better lose that edjicated sound if you want to last on the streets. The other lads won't be so nice if they think ye're too uppity fer 'em."

"That obvious, huh?"

Henry laughed. "Ya may not look it just now, but ya sound like a swell."

"Thanks for telling me." Young Henry was a know-it-all if he'd ever met one.

"See that sundries shop two doors up the street? There's a warehouse behind it, and they need someone to move things in and out. Stuff's too big fer me, or I could've had the job. If ya'd like, I can take ya down there and talk to the boss fer ya."

"Why would you do that for me?" Nat asked. Queer sort of boy.

"Well, maybe I feel sorry for ya, standing there all covered in dust."

"I don't need anyone feeling—"

Before he could finish, Henry interrupted, "I'll be back," and he ran into the shop. In a moment he returned with a whisk broom and commenced to brush the dust off Nat's blue coat.

"Just a minute. I can take care of myself," Nat blustered.

"Yeah, anyone can see that." Henry continued to broom off the dust. "Got to spiff ya up before we go see Mr. Mullins. He's a nice man, and I expect ya to do a good job if I'm ter take ya to 'im."

When Henry had finished sweeping, he took a grimy kerchief from his pocket, spit on it, and rubbed a dirty spot on Nat's face.

"Here, now," Nat said as he backed away from Henry. "You're acting like my mother."

"You have a mum?" Henry asked.

"Of course I do. Everyone does, you ninny."

"I mean, is she alive?" Henry probed.

"Yes, she is," Nathan said. Guilt gripped him as he thought of what she must be going through because of him. He had a way of breaking her heart.

"Then why are ya here on the street? If I had a mum, I wouldn't be here, I can tell ya," Henry said.

"It's a long story." He patted Henry's shoulder.

"Well, we ain't got time fer stories now. Maybe later. I'll take ya to Mullins and see if we can fix ya up." Henry started down the street at a trot with Nat behind him.

Mr. Mullins sat at his desk in his shirtsleeves, going through a stack of papers. A pudgy man with thinning hair brushed over his nearly bald head, he looked up as the boys entered.

"I've brought ya a new warehouse man, Mr. Mullins," said Henry. "His name is Nathan. I think he can do the job for ya."

Mr. Mullins put down his pen. He stood and walked around his desk, all the while looking Nat over.

"Let me see your muscles, boy."

Nat rolled up his sleeve and flexed his arm.

"Are you willing to work hard?"

"Yes, sir," said Nat.

"Well, since Henry vouches for you, I'll give you a try. Part of yer wages will be a room and a bed in my warehouse. There will be one hot meal a day at two in the afternoon. The rest, ye're on yer own." He reached out his hand, and Nat took it in a firm grasp.

There was a place to stay, thought Nat, and one meal a day, all thanks to Henry. Now, where had the lad gone? The wage was only a pittance next to his allowance, but it was better than he'd scraped together with odd jobs over the last week he'd been in hiding.

Mr. Mullins took Nat through the warehouse to the loading dock in the back.

"Here the drays bring in the merchandise, and you and the driver will unload them. You'll be responsible for putting the merchandise in place in the warehouse and later in the shop when it is needed. I hurt my back and can no longer lift the heavy boxes. This is your room. There's a cot, a small chest for yer clothes, and a large bowl for washing over there. You'll be responsible for keeping this room clean. I don't want no rats and such making their home in my warehouse."

Nat nodded his head. "Yes, sir."

"Well, Nathan, let's get to work. I'll show you where the different boxes go. The driver'll bring his cart anytime now."

The sweat ran down Nat's face, and his hands were scratched and blistered from moving boxes, but he was thankful for the work. A pain in his belly told him it was time to eat.

A cheerful voice called from the shop, and Mr. Mullins shouted back, "Here in the warehouse."

The fragrance of the meat pie entered the room before the woman carrying it. She was as pudgy as her husband, and her eyes twinkled in her cheerful round face.

"Here's your lunch, Mr. Mullins, and have ye got someone to help ye? I dare say there will be plenty for the two o' ye."

"This is Nathan. I hired him earlier. He's worked hard this morning, and I am sure he's ready to dig into that pie, Mrs. Mullins."

"Well, I'll cut ye off a good slice and put it on this tin plate fer ye. There ye go, boy," she said as she handed it to Nathan.

Mr. and Mrs. Mullins went into the shop, and Nat took his plate to his room.

That night as he lay on his cot, Nat thought about his family. His mother would be worrying and praying. Father too. He pulled the cover up around his shoulders. The night was cold, but the chill he felt was from fear. Nighttime was the worst. He had lost everything: family, home, friends. Maybe . . . maybe his life if the Runners found him. A wave of nausea pinched his belly. They hanged murderers, didn't they? The dread that started in his belly rose to his throat like bile, leaving a bitter taste in his mouth.

He tried to stretch. The muscles in his arms and shoulders ached. He reached under the blanket and rubbed his calves to get the kinks out. At least he had this job and a place to sleep at night. He would thank Henry tomorrow.

"Nathan" had been working for a week when Mr. Mullins called him to his office. "I can see ye're willing to work and have a brain in yer head. I'd like you to help me with the inventory."

Nat replied, "Glad to. What do you want done?"

Mr. Mullins took him into the warehouse and showed him how to count the merchandise from each of his suppliers and write it down in the accounting book.

Henry came through the back door of the warehouse as the shop was closing that evening.

"I see ye're fit and a whole lot cleaner than the first time I saw ya," said Henry with a snicker.

Nat glanced up from where he was working. "Well, hello. I didn't hear you come in. You're looking cocksure of yourself."

"I was right, wasn't I? I can see he has ya doin' the inventory already. This job was made fer ya. Mr. Mullins'll have ya runnin' the place in no time."

Nat laughed. "I doubt that, but I do thank you for your help. I owe you a big favor for this."

"Don't be such a gabster. Ye needed work, and Mr. Mullins needed help." Henry's cheeks colored slightly as he said it. "I'll bet ye're enjoyin' Mrs. Mullins' meals. She has a sister who lives on a farm in the country, and she sends food in every week. I've had a bit o' lunch 'ere a time or two." There was a look of longing on his face as he talked about the food.

The boy did look like he wasn't getting enough to eat. "Would you believe she brought us muffins today, and I have one left? I was thinking about getting something from the pie man for my supper, so I won't need it. Would you like the muffin? It has currants in it." Nat watched Henry's eyes grow big.

"Well, if ye're sure ya don't want it." Henry smiled.

When Nat handed it to the boy, he could almost see Henry's mouth water. "Why don't you eat it now, since I have no napkin to put it on."

He ate it slowly, deliberately chewing each bite and savoring the last crumb. Funny way for a boy to eat, thought Nat. Most would have gobbled it down in two bites.

Next morning Nat pulled back the doors to the dock and heard some shouting. A yell of pain sent him from the dock in a leap. Down the alleyway he could see boys scuffling, and it appeared one was getting the worst of it.

"Let go of it!" one yelled.

"Hit him again!" shouted another.

"Ya can't have it. It's mine!" That voice was Henry's.

Nat arrived in time to separate the boys before any more damage was done. Three of them scampered off. Henry lay sprawled on his backside with a bloody nose and a small leather purse tightly clutched in his fingers.

Nat took his handkerchief and staunched the flow of blood from the pug nose. He'd never noticed how small it was before or the freckles running across it.

"What was that all about, Henry?"

"They were tryin' . . . to steal my purse." He gulped down a sob.

"Do you know them?" Nat asked.

"They're a scruffy bunch, always causing trouble." His breath came in gasps. "I saw 'em stealing yesterday from the shop."

Nat pulled him up from the dirt. "Are you all right now?"

"I think so." He straightened his clothes. "Thanks for the help and the kerchief. I guess we're even now."

"I guess we are, but I want to walk home with you this evening to make sure those hooligans don't bother you again."

"Nah, I'll be fine."

"I would like to make sure. Besides, I think I should know where you live, in case I ever need to find you."

Henry picked his cap off the ground and pulled it down on his forehead. "I can take care of meself." He brushed his clothes off and stuffed the bloody kerchief into his pocket. "Thanks again for the help," he said over his shoulder as he entered the back door of the shop. "It's getting late, and Mr. Thomas will be here soon."

"I'll be watching just the same, Henry, my boy," Nat murmured.

Nat got his work done early and waited at the side of the building as Henry walked by, crossed the street, and turned the corner. Nat followed at a distance. He had heard the lad lived with his aunt and uncle, so he was surprised when Henry turned into a street of old, deserted warehouses. Hidden in a doorway, he watched the boy look around and disappear into one of the buildings. Nat looked in the boarded window through a knothole. He saw a large room with a small door in the right wall. It was obvious Henry didn't want anyone to know where he lived. The boy was on his own, probably hiding that fact to stay out of the orphanage. How many of the children he saw working on the streets were without families and homes? How could he help them? He thought of his own home and the parents who had always loved and protected him. He'd been a lucky young man.

Chapter Fifteen

Deverell bought a meat pie from a man on the street. He dared not think what was in it, but he was hungry and in a hurry. He asked the seller, "Do you know where I might find someone who sells red roses?"

"You're probably wantin' Gertie. She has a flower stall at the marketplace two streets down and two to yer left. But she ain't there now, guv'ner. She starts at sunrise and leaves as soon as she sells 'em all. She'll be back to sell to the gents in the evening."

Dev returned to the factory to tell his father, "I'll go back this evening to find the woman."

The lamplighters were out, and from his cab he could hear the voices of the vendors crying "Buy my pies" and "Shoelaces fer sale." Laborers from the nearby factories shuffled into the narrow streets with heads down and faces drawn. A few streets over, men in top hats spilled out of business offices, shouting for cabs above the cacophony of sound.

"Let me out here, driver," Deverell called.

His mind on finding the flower seller, he pressed through the crowds. Ahead he saw a young girl with nosegays of bright flowers in a box held around her neck by a strap.

"A posy for your missus, sir?"

"Is your name Gertie?"

"Nah, guv'ner. I'n't my flowers good enuf fer ya?"

"They're very nice, but I need to speak to Gertie. Can you tell me where she would be at this time of evening?"

"You can find 'er down two blocks and over three more, where the toffs are. She 'as a lot of regular customers, she does."

"Thanks, miss." He threw a coin into the box and started up the street.

The girl called, "Thanks, guv'ner."

It was a busy evening for a Monday, and Gertie was selling a bouquet to a swell of the first stare when Deverell approached her.

"Flowers, sir?" she asked.

"Are you Gertie?"

"Might be. Why do ye ask?" Curiosity glistened in her eyes.

"Do you sell flowers in the marketplace early in the morning?"

"Who are ya?" The tone was belligerent.

"I'm not a Runner, if that's what you're thinking. I've an important question to ask about a bunch of red roses that you sold last Tuesday morning early. Do you remember that morning?"

"I'll try, if it's important."

"It is," Deverell said.

"I remember the day, 'cause there'd been a downpour the night afore, and I were afraid me flowers might be ruin't, but they was fine. I sold several bunches to me regulars, and then there was the bunch I sold to a fine gentleman that comes around occasional-like. He came early, just after sunrise."

"Do you know his name?"

"Nah, but I can tell you what he looks like. He rides a black horse. He's tall and dresses like a swell. He buys flowers from me 'bout every fortnight. Usually they're violets, but that day he wanted red roses."

Deverell took a card from his pocket and handed it to her, along with a half crown. "If you think of anything else you can tell me about this man, there will be more where that came from. Ask for Mr. Deverell Bromfield at that address. It is very important that I find the man you described."

The girl's eyes lit up at the sight of the money. "I'll do me best, sir."

A tall gentleman on a black horse—how many men like that were in London and its surrounding countryside? Disappointment thinned his lips as he hailed a cab. He had just enough time to meet his father for dinner.

The next morning when he prepared to leave, his father clasped his shoulder. "Find him, Deverell. Find Nat."

Deverell hugged him. "I will, Father, I promise. I'll bring him home safe and sound." But how was he going to do it?

Deverell procured one of the sketches from Bow Street. It was a good likeness of Nat. He questioned street vendors and shopkeepers along an alleyway. "I'm not with the police, but I'm looking for a friend who disappeared a week ago. Here's a picture of him." The majority shook their heads no; a few asked if there was a reward.

Deverell looked at his pocket watch. Five hours he'd searched with no hint of success. Most of the time he had led his horse through a crush of people. His legs were tired and aching. Riding boots weren't made for walking on filth-strewn streets. The orange he'd bought from an old woman earlier could not stave off his hunger any longer. He needed a real meal. A drop of rain on his hand, then another, sent his gaze to the cloudy sky. He made a run for the inn ahead and left his horse in the attached stable. Inside, he removed his hat and brushed the rain from it and the shoulders of his coat. A middle-aged man with a wide, ingratiating smile that showed his stained teeth stood by the door.

"Let me take your coat and hat, sir."

Fatigue and hunger had set in, but Deverell asked about Nat first. "Landlord, have you seen this young man?"

"I don't remember him, sir, but my daughter, Susannah, might. She's in the back. I'll send her to ye," the man said. "Are ye looking for a room?"

"Yes. Take my valise and put it in my room while I talk to your daughter."

"Yer room will be up the stairs and at the end of the hall on the left, sir."

The buxom young woman gazed at Deverell with large blue eyes, her mouth drawn up in a bow as she came through the door from the back room. "My papa says you want to ask me a question?" She gave him an appraising look.

He handed her the picture and asked, "Have you seen this man? He may have come this way about a week ago."

"You don't look like no Runner. They were here asking about him a while back. I didn't tell them nothin'. What do ye want to know fer?"

"He's a friend, and he disappeared near here," Deverell told her. "I'm not a constable or Bow Street Runner."

"What color are his eyes?" she asked with an impertinent grin.

"You tell me," Deverell replied. "I have the feeling you are very observant." *Especially if it's a man.*

"They was dark brown. He were real nervous-like. Polite enuf but in a hurry to get to his room. He asked me to bring up some food. Wouldn't open the door 'til I told him who I was. He wasn't very tall. Had a baby face, the kind women like, if you know what I mean."

"Which way did he go when he left?" Deverell asked. "Think carefully, please—this is very important."

"He left very early, barely light out. I was helping me father, so I saw him leave. He went that way, walking fast." She pointed east. "London's a big town, and a man can get lost here if he tries."

He took her hand and laid some coins in it. He smiled. "Thank you." At last, an indication he was going in the right direction. His stomach reminded him with a low rumble of his hunger.

Her eyes sparkling, Susannah watched the man walk toward the stairs. Now, there went a real gentleman, and a looker. She smiled as her gaze roved from his broad shoulders over his well-proportioned body, down to his muscular legs.

Feet hurting from the uneven cobblestone streets and the throb of a headache brought another day of fruitless searching to an end. Deverell massaged his temples to ease the pain and sighed at the thought of staying in the run-down establishment up ahead. Dirt ran down the walls in rivulets from the rain, and the shingles had fallen off one corner of the roof. Still, it was the best he had seen since coming into this poorer section of London. No one greeted him to take his horse, so he rode into the lean-to they used as a stable. A young boy emerged from one of the stalls and took the reins. He was shabbily dressed and dirty, but he held a piece of carrot out to the horse, who took it daintily from his fingers.

Deverell handed him the reins. "She needs to be rubbed down and fed, young man."

"Yes, sir." The boy pulled his forelock.

"This is for you," he said, handing him a coin, "and there'll be more if you take good care of my mount."

"I will, sir," he said, and he bit the coin before he shoved it into his pocket.

The light rain had dampened Deverell's spirits and his clothes. His muscles ached, and he was chilled to the bone. He hurried into the inn and out of the weather.

The portly man behind the desk asked, "Can I help you, sir?"

"I'll need a room and a bath for tonight," Deverell said, and he removed his hat and brushed off the raindrops.

The man's owlish eyes rested upon Deverell's finely tied neck cloth and the excellent cut of his coat. "Yes, sir, my very best room will be yours, and a fine meal as well in a private dining room."

"I'm looking for this man. He's a friend of mine. Have you seen him in the last fortnight?" asked Deverell, holding out the police sketch.

The man gave him a quizzical look and, setting his glasses firmly on his bulbous nose, examined the drawing.

"I can't say that I have." He continued to stare at it. "No, I'm sure I haven't seen him."

Disappointed, Deverell thanked the man. "Show me to my room."

The innkeeper took Deverell's valise and led the way up the dimly lit stairs to the "very best" room. The man lit a lamp, and flickering light revealed a large four-poster bed and a bureau.

"Would you like the fire lit, sir?"

"Please." Musty air assailed his nose when he walked into the room. The wallpaper was water-stained and peeling in one corner near the ceiling. Deverell threw the covers on the bed back to look at the linens. Thank goodness they were clean.

"I'll send a boy up with a tub and some hot water, sir," the man said before he closed the door.

A week on the road made him glad for even a room like this one. Deverell sat on the edge of the bed and pulled off his boots. A bath and a good dinner and he'd feel like a new man.

"I wonder how many miles I've traveled. That boy has led me a merry chase," he mumbled to himself. "I daresay he's used his brain, though, to stay out of the Runners' grasp."

Dinner was passable, though a bit greasy. Glad to crawl into bed and stretch out his weary body, Dev found his mind filled with Nat again. The boy would be running out of money and would need to find work in order to survive. "When I find him, I'll box his ears for putting me to all this trouble." A smile crossed his lips.

He drifted into a light doze, and the face of Alexandra replaced his worry for Nat. Warmth crept through him, and he could smell the lavender fragrance she wore. A deeper relationship with her was worth pursuing, but there was something he had to do first. Get Nat out of trouble.

The odor of the slimy muck running down the gutters assailed Deverell's nostrils. He covered his nose with a handkerchief. The dismal little shacks that stood jammed together with taverns and brothels caught his attention. How did these people survive?

"Careful, Bess," he murmured to his horse as she picked her way through costermongers trundling carts of wilted and spoiling produce, and people with wheelbarrows full of all kinds of rubbish. Could they be oblivious to the stench?

Three young men leaned against the wall of a noisy tavern and gave him a hard look as he rode past. Summing up the worth of the money in his purse and the clothes on his back, no doubt. A creeping shiver of fear ran down his spine, and perspiration wet his armpits. He had to find his brother soon, but in the meantime he needed to blend in better with the people here. At the first opportunity in the narrow street, he turned his horse around and headed back to the small hotel where he'd stayed the night before.

The owner met him with a look of delight. "Welcome back, sir. Will you be needing a room again?" His smile widened in his pockmarked face.

Deverell gave him a nod. "Do you have a secondhand clothes shop nearby?" he asked.

"Certainly, sir. It will be to your left as you go out and down two blocks."

Deverell removed his hat and greatcoat and gave them to the man. "Please take these and my bag to my room, and I will need some hot water for a bath when I return."

The innkeeper met him as he returned from his shopping. "The maid will be on her way to your room soon. Would you like a glass of cold cider while you wait, sir?"

"Bring it to my room, please."

"Right away, sir."

The owner's smile and effusive manners told Deverell that he loved having a swell in the hotel, no doubt because swells were typically free with their blunt.

The next morning, fog overlaid the city and trapped all the smoke beneath it. Deverell stepped out into the brown gloom and immediately reached for his handkerchief, only to remember he no longer carried it. No matter; it would not have gone with his patched jacket and threadbare shirt. The pants came to his ankles, and the shoes were worn, the laces broken. He'd tied his small leather purse around his neck under his shirt, away from prying eyes. He smiled at the thought of one of his friends or, heaven forbid, his mother seeing him dressed like this.

Across the street a tall blond man slouched against the door frame watching the entrance to the hotel. It was past ten o'clock, and his stomach rumbled with hunger.

"Where is he? He usually starts out earlier than this." The man spoke to himself, twisting the ring on his little finger. He didn't understand why Deverell had come back so early yesterday. It didn't make sense. Surely he was getting close to finding the boy. When he'd decided to follow Dev, he felt sure Dev would lead him to Nat. He had not come all this way to lose Bromfield now.

It had not occurred to Lucian that the disheveled and dirty man who had left the hotel by way of the alley was the debonair and dashing Mr. Deverell Bromfield.

Deverell leaned against a building, slipped one foot out of its shoe, and rubbed the red spot on his heel. He dreaded putting the old shoe back on. He caught a glimpse of two small boys, no older than four or five. The older reached out to grab his shoe, and Deverell put his foot down firmly on top to keep the child from snatching it. As the child pulled back, he saw the boy's eyes—old and hopeless, in a dirt-smudged face. Both boys ran away on spindly legs bowed by rickets.

He had never seen such filth and hungry desperation. If he had not needed the shoe to continue his search, he would have gladly given it and much more to them. His heart ached for the children. What could be done? There were so many.

He eased the shoe on and looked for the nearest gin shop, hoping he could pick up some news there. The small dark room he ambled into smelled of sweaty bodies, sour beer, and some other things he did not recognize.

"A small glass of beer." He threw a coin down and gazed around the room.

"Only got gin. Don't sell no beer 'ere." The shopkeeper gave Deverell a sullen look.

"I'll take the gin, then. Heard of a job anywhere?"

"Ye're not from 'ere or ye'd know there i'n't no work but scavenging round 'ere. Ye best go on a ways. There's warehouses, shops, and the like farther on."

Deverell put the glass to his lips and set it down untouched. "How far?"

"Go down ta the corner and turn right and go 'alf a mile ta the main road. About a two-hour walk after that."

Deverell took out the picture of Nat and showed it to the barman. "I been lookin' fer this man. Did you see him about two weeks ago?"

"I maight, and then again I maight not. What's it worf to ye?"

"Tell me the color of his eyes, and I'll letcha know." Deverell kept his impatience under control.

"They was brown, like his 'air. 'E was young and didn't belong around 'ere."

"That's him." Deverell kept the excitement out of his voice. "Where'd he go?"

"Let me see the color of yer money first."

Deverell took out one of the few coins he had tucked in the pocket of his jacket. He laid it on the bar.

"I give 'im the same advice I give you," the man said as he slid his pudgy hand over the money.

Nat stuck his head out of the back door of the shop warehouse and smiled to see that it was neither foggy nor raining this evening. How he missed the fresh air of the country. Not much of that in London. He'd get his jacket and take a walk. He locked the door behind him and turned into the alley, when a strong arm grabbed him from behind and a hand went over his mouth.

"Well, at last I have caught you," a husky voice said.

Chapter Sixteen

A chill ran over Nat, and he broke into a cold sweat as he struggled to free himself. He swung a leg back, trying to trip his attacker and at the same time gave him a swift elbow to the ribs.

"No, you don't, gudgeon. It's me, Deverell."

Breathing heavily and still wary, Nat turned around to see a disheveled, dirty character with a cap pulled down to his eyes.

"What the . . . ?"

The man removed the cap and stepped into a pool of light from a streetlamp. Sure enough, his brother looked back at him.

"It's me, Nat, your brother."

Nat grabbed his neck and hugged him, then moved back. "I could whip you for scaring me like that."

"Sorry, I guess I overdid it. Is there someplace we can go to talk? We don't want to arouse any curiosity."

"I have a room inside."

Nat led Deverell through the warehouse to his room. He lit a candle and held it up to his brother's face. He started to laugh. "You've come down in the world since I last saw you."

Deverell looked around the tiny room with its cot and small chest. "Haven't we all? Although this looks better than the last room I stayed in."

Nat motioned for his brother to sit down on the bed. He sat on the floor and leaned against the wall. Seeing Deverell here gave him hope that he might yet get out of this mess.

Deverell removed his shoes and rubbed his tender feet. He

winced as he discovered a large blister on his heel. The candle-light also revealed the weariness in his face.

"I'll make a bandage for that," Nat offered quickly.

"The morning will be soon enough," said Deverell.

Curious, Nat asked, "How did you find me?"

"I asked a lot of questions and laid out some blunt. A man in a gin shop told me you had asked for work, and he had sent you in this direction. I kept my eyes open, and there you were, unloading a dray this morning. I stayed around until I could find you alone."

"Are the police still looking for me?" He couldn't keep the fear out of his voice.

"They were when I left a week ago. Haven't seen any Robin Redbreasts, have you?"

"No Horse Patrol has been in this neighborhood." Nat pulled his knees up and wrapped his arms around them. "What am I going to do, Dev?"

"Tell me what happened."

"I came to London to see Leticia and to explain about the fight at Stanhope's. I hadn't eaten anything for hours, and when she offered me some port, I drank it. You know how I am. It went straight to my brain. It'd been raining hard before I got to her house, and I was drenched. She gave me a robe to put on, and when I came out of the dressing room, she kissed me."

Nat's face turned red, and he dropped his gaze.

"She is, ah, was, a tempting armful, and I was in over my head. I had another glass of port, and that is the last thing I remember."

He looked at Deverell, his eyes pleading. "I'm not making excuses for my behavior. That's just the way it was. When I awoke the next morning, I left as quickly as I could dress and went to get my things at the livery. I took a room at the nearest hotel. I swear she was alive when I left her house."

"I didn't think you had harmed her. I know you too well for that." Deverell smiled at him. "I did some investigating on my own before I left to look for you. Did you take her roses that night?"

"I didn't take her anything."

"Well, someone did, and it must have been early in the morning after you left and before the housekeeper came in. She found them in the dustbin the next morning."

"But who? Who else was there?"

"That's what I'm trying to find out. Whoever brought them must have been the murderer."

"Stanhope? He would certainly have the motive, if he thought she and I were, well, you know."

Deverell's shoulders sagged. "I suppose we must consider him. I have a hard time believing he could do such a thing, but he would have a motive. They found your monogrammed handkerchief in her boudoir."

"How did they know it was mine? I didn't give my name."

"They showed it to Stanhope, and he gave the constable your name. Mother identified it as yours."

"Mother? Oh, no." Nat clenched his jaw and squeezed his eyes shut. "What have I done to my family?"

"Father's taking it pretty well. He's worried, of course. Mother's praying."

Nat nodded. "I knew she would."

"I think the best thing for you to do is to stay here and just continue as you have been. Try to stay out of trouble. Now, is there anything around here to eat? I am fair gut-founded." Deverell yawned.

"I have some bread left from lunch, and I can make us a pot of tea on the stove in the back of the shop. I'll see what else I can find. You wait here."

Nat jumped up and reached for the bread covered with a napkin on top of the chest. He handed it to his brother. Dev took the bread, then grasped his brother's arm. "Glad you are safe, little brother."

Nat held his brother's gaze, then took down a small lantern from the nail by the door, lit it, and left the room.

When he returned with the tea, the bread was gone, and his brother was dozing. Nat had found some biscuits and an orange.

He shook Deverell's shoulder. "Here, you'd better eat this,

and then you can have a proper rest." He poured the tea into a tin cup and handed it to him.

"Thanks, Nat," Deverell said, "but where will you sleep?"

"I'll be fine here with the extra blanket."

He lay on the floor and propped up his elbow, leaning his head on his hand. He watched Dev, and a sense of relief and safety swept over him. His big brother always came through for him. Tonight he would sleep deeply.

Nat awoke early the next morning. He looked down at Dev, and his heart tightened with love as he shut the door. The dray would be there soon with a load of boxes for him to put away. His steps quickened as he hurried out to get some breakfast.

On his return, he woke Deverell with a touch on the arm. "There's a bowl of water and a towel. You can get a cup of tea and a good pudding with currants at the little hostelry down the street for breakfast. Tell anyone who asks you are David, an acquaintance of mine. That shouldn't arouse anyone's curiosity."

Deverell stretched and opened his mouth in a wide yawn. "I haven't slept this well in days. What time is it?"

"The sun's up, and I have to go to work soon. I'll share my lunch with you at two."

When Nat brought the large piece of meat pie into his room that afternoon, Deverell was lounging on the cot. "What's that heavenly smell?"

"Mrs. Mullins' savory meat pie."

"And here I'd been worrying that you were starving."

Nat chuckled as he divided the pie and gave half to Deverell along with a mug of cider.

Nat sat on the floor and looked up at his brother. "What are we going to do now?" There was expectancy in his eyes.

Deverell saw the trust and prayed he would be able to help his brother. "I'm going home. Mother and Father will be anxious to hear you are safe. When I return to London, I'll continue to look for who was at Leticia's that morning after you left. Someone must have seen something. I'll talk to the flower seller again. You keep an eye out for any strangers. Stay in as much as you can. If I leave now, I can be back at the hotel before dark."

There was a knock on the door. "Nathan, are ya in there?"

"Nathan?" Deverell mouthed to Nat.

"That's me," Nat whispered back. "It's a young lad I know, Henry. I'll introduce you as a friend." He opened the door.

"Hello, Henry. You've come by early today."

"I finished my job and just stopped by to see how ye're doin'. I didn't mean ta interrupt yer visitin'."

"This is a friend of mine, David."

"Glad ter meetcha, David. Nice of ya to visit Nathan. How long are ya here fer?"

"Nice to meet you too, Henry. I have to leave in a few minutes."

"Well, I best be goin' and let ya say yer farewells. See ya, Nathan." Henry shut the door behind him.

Deverell was curious. "Where did you meet Henry?"

"I was sleeping in the doorway of the shop he was working in, and he swept dirt all over me. I guess he felt sorry for me, because he helped me get this job."

Deverell frowned. What was there about the boy that disturbed him? He couldn't quite put his finger on it.

"I discovered he lives alone, so I watch out for him when I can." Nat's face became serious. "There are a lot of young lads on their own here on the streets. It's a wonder how they make it."

How did he get past him? Lucian drew his brows together. Deverell's horse was still in the livery, so he'd left on foot. *He's got to come back. But if he has already found Nat, I'll be no better off than I was before.*

There was a knock on Lucian's door.

"Who's there?" he called.

"The maid, sir."

He opened the door to the delightful sight of a slender young miss with a pert smile and sparkling blue eyes. Her short blond curls peeked out from under her white mobcap.

"I've never seen you here before," Lucian said, his gaze appraising her boldly.

"That's because I only work two days a week. The mistress wants to know if you'll be here for supper."

"If you are serving, I'll be here," he said with a devastating smile.

"I'll be serving." She curtsied and turned away to tap on another guest's door.

Lucian watched the girl down the hall, then shut the door. He walked across the room and sat at the window, gazing into the twilight at the hotel across the street. His thoughts were on another woman. He had loved her, and she had proved faithless.

A muscle tightened his jaw, and he struck his thigh with his clenched fist, muttering, "She was a tantalizing witch."

His elbows on the arms of the chair, he held his head in his hands. A low moan from deep inside escaped his lips.

Chapter Seventeen

Anne Louise Bromfield's straw hat protected her fair skin as she walked through the garden with a pair of scissors in her hand and a basket on her arm.

She cut several blooms and gathered enough herbs for the kitchen before she sat on the bench near the sundial and placed her clippings beside her. With a sigh she pulled her white shawl about her shoulders against the chill in the late-afternoon air.

The greater chill was inside her heart. Surely Deverell would be back soon with news of Nat. Her shoulders drooped, and a single tear ran down her cheek. She could not believe the police thought her son had killed that woman. It was not possible. The crunch of gravel alerted her to her husband's approach.

"Fredrick, you're home at last." She rose, and his arms enfolded her. Anne Louise buried her head in his chest and felt some of the tension melt as his strength surrounded her.

"Have you seen Deverell?" Her soft voice had a catch in it.

"No, my dear. I would have come home sooner, but there was work I had to finish at the factory. I was hoping Deverell would return before I left." Mr. Bromfield touched her cheek and brushed away a tear. He kissed her gently, not caring if the servants saw. "We shall weather this storm, my dear."

Lucian watched as Deverell rode out of the livery and headed in the direction of the city. If the man was heading home, it meant he had found his brother. Lucian followed him on foot for a few blocks. Tomorrow he would start searching for Nathaniel himself. He didn't look forward to it, but with Deverell gone, he wouldn't have to worry about being seen.

He threw his clothes into his valise and set his hat firmly on his head. He was tired of spending his days waiting. Galahad would be glad for some exercise, and so would he. He could pick up the scent of the trail by asking about Deverell as well as showing the picture of Nat. He would find the boy, but first he would find an acceptable place for a room and a meal tonight.

Deverell rubbed Queen Bess' neck as the house came into view. "Home at last, girl." It was good to have his own clothes back, especially the boots, but he would feel much better after a good hot bath. Bess twitched her ears at his sigh and hastened her gait.

Anne Louise hurried to the door as soon as she heard Deverell's voice. "Have you found Nat? Is he safe?" Her red-rimmed eyes were full of hope.

Deverell hugged her and whispered in her ear, "Yes, to both questions, but do not ask me where he is. It is better you do not know."

His father heard voices and came down the hall. "I thought I heard your voice, son. Did you find him?"

Dev's heart ached when he saw his father's face etched with lines he had not seen before. "Shall we go into your study?"

The three hastened into the room, and Deverell closed the door. "It is better that the servants do not hear. I can tell you he is fine; there is no need to worry on that account. I will not tell you where he is or how I found him. The less you know, the better, in case the constable should question you again. Nat told me what happened that night. I'm following a lead or two, and I will see his name cleared. I'm going to ride over to see Stanhope later. I've not talked to him since it happened. But first I would like to clean up, and I'm famished for a home-cooked meal, Mother."

"I'll check with Cook and see when dinner will be ready."

His father pulled him aside. "Dev, are you going to ask

Stanhope where he was when Leticia was murdered? I know he's your close friend, but he was her lover, and clearly she wasn't honest with him."

"That is one of the things I am going to find out tonight—as much as I don't want to think he might have killed her."

Deverell tried to enjoy the meal, but thoughts of Stanhope and the upcoming conversation spoiled his enjoyment of it.

Deverell took one of his father's mares. Queen Bess deserved a long rest. On the ride his mind gnawed on the same old questions. Stanhope had the motive, but did he have the opportunity? His groom might shed some light on where his master had been the night of the murder. Could he get the man to tell him?

He rode directly to the stable yard, where the groom met him. "Good evening, Mr. Bromfield. I am sure Mr. Stanhope will be glad to see ye."

A guilty twinge pricked Deverell's conscience, "Yes, I am eager to see him too. I haven't talked to him in a while. Has he been in London lately?"

"He was there for a few days about a week ago."

"I've been busy in the factory. I thought he came to town the week before."

"Maybe so. He was gone for a few days. I'll be puttin' yer horse in the stable, sir."

Deverell let out a heavy sigh. Stanhope *was* gone from home that week.

The butler brought him into the study. "I shall see if Mr. Stanhope is available, Mr. Bromfield."

Deverell strolled around the room, looking at the portraits on the walls of Stanhope's father with his hunting dogs and horses. He read the titles of the books on the shelves. Anything to distract his mind from the conversation he would soon have with his friend.

The door opened, and Deverell could hear Fielding instructing the butler to bring them something to eat.

"There you are, Dev." Stanhope took his hand. "Good to see you. How have you been?"

"More to the point, Stanhope, how are you?" Deverell gave his friend a searching look.

"Fair. It's been a hellish two weeks." Stanhope motioned Deverell to a chair, and he took one nearby. "Would you like a drink?"

"No, thanks," Deverell said.

"I shall have one." Stanhope went to a small cabinet and took out a decanter. He poured amber liquid into a crystal glass, spilling some on the rug. He cursed under his breath. "This is not easy, Dev. After all, it is your brother they say killed her."

"You can't possibly believe that Nat killed Leticia." Deverell was astounded.

"Why not? He was there. They have the evidence." Stanhope leaned against the mahogany desk.

"That does not mean he killed her. What motive could he have?"

"She spurned his advances, and he killed her in a moment of rage. You know he has a temper." He set the glass beside him.

"Yes, but never toward women; he would not have killed Leticia. He couldn't have."

"Tell that to the magistrate."

Deverell rose and pointed a finger at his friend. "You had more motive than Nat had. No one likes to be betrayed."

Stanhope's face filled with rage, and he balled his hands into fists. "The only thing that keeps me from laying you flat is our long friendship. Now, if you would please oblige me by leaving my house, I would be most grateful."

"Please, I should not have spoken so."

"In case you would like to know where I was at the time of the murder, I had taken my mother to visit her cousin, and we were nowhere near London. You may ask her, and I will give you the name and address of our relative. I have already given it to that Constable Billings."

"We have been friends for a long time, Stanhope. I don't really believe you killed Leticia, but neither can I believe that Nat did it. You must understand that."

"He is your brother, and I can see how difficult this must be for your family, but who else could have done it? He was in her home that night."

"I talked to the housekeeper and some others. Their information leads me to believe someone entered the house after my brother left. Her housekeeper told me she saw other men when you were not in town. It could have been one of them."

Deverell winced at the crestfallen look on Stanhope's face, but it was his brother's life he was fighting for.

"I knew there were other men," Stanhope admitted. "Leticia was not the kind to be true to one man. She was so beautiful. It made you feel like someone when she was on your arm."

"I'm sorry, my friend, but do you know who any of them might have been?"

There was a knock on the door, and the butler entered with a tray.

"Put it here on the table, Williams."

Stanhope collapsed into a chair and stretched his legs out, his chin on his chest. He let out a great sigh and lifted his gaze to Deverell.

"I don't know who the other men were, although I had my suspicions from time to time. You know what she was like, always flirting. Who knew when she was serious?"

Deverell bounded to his feet and paced the floor. "I tried to warn Nat. He's a naive boy. How can you possibly think he killed her? You've known him since he was a child."

Stanhope stood. "You thought *I* did it, and *we* have been friends since childhood." He faced Deverell, his fists on his hips. "I suppose I'm still angry with him for the fight at my party."

"Well, are we still friends?"

"Of course, only I . . ." Stanhope lifted his hand and looked away.

"Well, out with it, man."

"I hired someone to find him."

"You what? You hired a professional?"

His eyes downcast, Stanhope said, "No, not exactly. I hired Lucian."

"Lucian? When did you hire him?"

"Several days ago. And I offered him a large sum of money if the boy is brought to justice."

"I can't believe you would do such a foolhardy thing." Deverell faced the fireplace. His hands gripped the mantel until his knuckles turned white. He struggled to breathe as a tight band of fear encased his chest.

"Bow Street wasn't doing anything. I thought he could help them out. He's always in dun territory, and I knew he could use the money," Stanhope said.

"I have to find Lucian before he finds Nat. The boy won't have a chance."

"I'm sorry. I guess I wasn't thinking straight."

The man looked so forlorn, Deverell reached out and grasped his shoulder. "We shall find the man who killed Leticia, but first I must make sure my brother is safe." He hurried from the room.

Stanhope fell back into the chair and picked up a slice of cold beef. He stared into space as he chewed without tasting, then washed it down with a glass of wine.

Chapter Eighteen

Deverell's father met him in the hallway on his return home. "There's a message I forgot to give you from the flower seller, Gertie. She came to the office with more information about the man who bought the roses." He rummaged through the papers on top of his desk. "Here it is. I wrote down what she said word for word: 'The man had fair hair. I remember the sun shining off it when he raised his hat. He wore a ring on his little finger that he kept fiddling with while he waited.'"

Dev took the message and reread it. "This will be helpful, Father. I hope you rewarded her well."

"She seemed pleased." His father raised an eyebrow and gave him a wry smile.

Dev mentally recited what he knew of the mystery man so far. Tall, fair hair, a black horse, and a ring he fiddled with on his little finger. He knew someone who did that. Lucian Moreton. But that was absurd. Still, could it possibly be Lucian? Lucian was out looking for Nat. If he were the murderer, would he kill Nat and then bring the police his body? But Lucian Moreton was his friend and Alexi's brother. He couldn't believe it of him. Yet . . .

"I'm going to the Moretons' in London tomorrow. It's important I see Alexi." Deverell clasped his father's shoulder. "I'll pack this evening."

"Call the valet to help you."

Late the next morning Deverell knocked on the door of the Moreton terrace home and was ushered in by the footman. "I should like to see Miss Alexandra, please."

A voice from down the hall called, "Is that Bromfield? Bring him to my office."

"Dr. Moreton, I know you are busy, but I need to see your daughter for a few minutes, if at all possible."

The man stood behind his desk. "I want to talk to you first, Deverell. It's come to my attention that you and Alexandra have been spending time with each other."

"That's correct, sir."

"I am afraid it's impossible for you to continue to do so. This situation with your brother must be hard for your family. I hesitate to add to your problems, but I cannot have my daughter's name connected with this kind of disgrace. I am sure you'll understand how I feel."

Deverell's eyes narrowed, and his jaw tightened. "How long do you think we should wait, sir?"

"It would be better if you did not see each other until this problem is resolved. Then I'll decide the best course of action."

"I don't want any scandal to touch Miss Alexandra either, sir, but my brother's innocent, and we'll prove it."

"I am sure you will, but I must protect my daughter."

Alexandra had a message from the footman that Deverell was in her father's office. She could hear her father's raised voice as she came down the stairs. What was the matter? Her skirts billowed around her as she hurried to the room.

Her father's flushed face was the first thing she saw as she opened the door. Deverell's back was as straight as a ramrod, his arms stiff at his sides.

"I beg your pardon, but I heard that Mr. Bromfield had come to see me." The sound of her voice caused Deverell to turn. There was a pained expression on his face.

"Have I interrupted something?" she asked, her hand still resting on the door handle.

"I have explained to Mr. Bromfield that the situation with his brother will make it impossible for you to continue seeing each other. That's all."

"That's all? I think you might have spoken to me first."

"Alexandra, this is for your own good. I won't have anything of this kind touching your name."

"I should like to talk to Deverell alone, please."

"For a few moments," said her father. "You may use this room."

"Thank you, Father."

Dr. Moreton left the door open.

Deverell took Alexandra's shaking hands in his. She heard him sigh and felt his breath against her cheek. Her eyes flashed with anger as she looked up at him.

"Dev, how could Father say those things to you, as if you did not have enough to bear already? Lucian told me about the newspaper article when he met Mother and me for tea several days ago."

He held her at arm's length. "What day did you see Lucian?"

"It was on a Tuesday, I believe. Yes, Tuesday, a week ago. I didn't tell him you were out of town looking for Nathaniel. Did you find him?"

"I can only tell you that Nat's all right. Have you seen Lucian since?"

"No, but why do you want to know about my brother?"

Deverell walked away. His back was to her as he looked at the books on the shelf. "I'll be leaving again tomorrow morning. I've an important errand," he said, his voice even.

"Do not try to hoax me. What does Lucian have to do with this?" She took his arm and turned him so she could see what was in his eyes.

"Stanhope hired him to find Nat."

She frowned. "Why?"

"To turn him over to the police," Deverell answered.

Her hand clutched his arm. "Stanhope believes that Nathaniel killed the woman?"

"He did. I don't think he does now. Tomorrow I start the search for Lucian to stop him from turning my brother in to the law."

"I'll help you."

"Help me? I don't see how, Alexi. I am going to a very poor part of London, and it is not safe for a woman. Besides, it could take days to find him. No, you can't go with me. Your father would have my head."

She turned from him to hide her disappointment.

Dev put his hands on her waist and lay his head next to hers. She leaned against him and inhaled his sandalwood scent. He laid his cheek against her hair.

"It's too dangerous," he whispered.

She turned and faced him, her hands on his chest. "I know Lucian better than anyone. I can help you find him. He'll listen to me. Please, Dev, he's my brother."

"No, Alexi, you are not going, and that is my final word." He stopped her protest with a soft kiss on her lips and left the room.

The next morning Deverell went early to his office to tell his clerk he would be out of town for a few days. He checked the stack of papers on his desk for any business he needed to complete before he left.

A small valise with an extra shirt and other necessities sat by the door. He carried it out to the factory stable, where his horse was saddled and waiting.

"There's a disreputable-looking boy inside who insists on seeing you, Mr. Bromfield. I've done everything but throw him out, and he still won't leave," said the stable hand.

"What does he want?"

"Says he won't talk to anyone but you, sir."

"Well, it's about time ya got here," said the young urchin with an impertinent thrust of his chin.

The stable boy stood in the open doorway staring at his boss with a questioning glance.

"I came to talk ter Mr. Bromfield," said the youth with a backward glance.

Deverell nodded to George, who backed out the door and closed it.

"Young man, if it's a job you've come for, you'll need to speak with Johnson. He does the hiring."

Deverell could see the youth's clothes were patched but clean. His cap was pulled down almost to his eyes, and the half boots were worn.

"I have a job. I'm your new groom, not a rag-picker, sir. Yer father hired me."

"My father? He never told me."

"Well, he told me. I have my pony, and I'll ride as your groom."

The boy was too smoky by half. What was he up to?

"I don't have time to argue with you. If you're coming with me, you'll have to keep up."

Dev raised his eyebrows and rolled his eyes when he saw the lad mount a fat cob. The boy rode behind him and kept up the pace, though the pony's sides were heaving. Deverell glanced back and slowed his pace. He called the lad to ride up beside him.

Hanging from underneath the boy's cap in the back was a long strand of auburn hair.

"I knew it." He reached over and pulled the cap off.

Alexi's shining curls spilled over the shoulders of her tattered jacket. He stopped his horse and turned her around by the shoulder.

"I fooled you for a while. What gave me away?" Her smile taunted him.

He picked up one of her long ringlets and gave it a gentle tug.

"I'll be more careful next time." She took her cap out of his hand and tucked her hair under it.

"Next time? Alexi, you're impossible." Exasperation was written on his face.

"It's a good idea, though—admit it."

He couldn't take her with him, but if he didn't, she would follow him, and that would be far more dangerous for her. Confound it. She'd given him no choice.

"It might work. What did you tell your parents?" Deverell asked.

"A friend from school invited me to stay with her for a few days. My mother was surprised, but Father assumed I wanted to get away because I was angry with him."

"You are too devious, my dear girl." His smile took the sting from the words.

She lowered her eyelashes and tried to look demure.

Deverell shook his head. "Let's go, boy. You'll need a name. I guess Alex will do."

Alexi bowed her head and shoved back an errant curl.

Dev placed the end of his whip under her chin and lifted her face. "Remember, I am the master. You are the groom."

Her eyes flashed a warning at his smiling face.

He grinned. "This should be interesting after all."

They rode in silence for a while. The pony bounced her along, and when she spoke, her voice sounded breathless. "How much farther have we to go?"

"We shall follow the same roads I took. There's a woman at the inn up ahead who remembered Nat. We can ask if Lucian stopped there too."

"Yes, sir." Alexi touched her cap.

At the inn, Deverell asked for the owner's daughter. Out of the corner of his eye he noticed the flush on Alexi's face when the buxom girl appeared with a bright smile for him.

"Well, sir, 'tis nice to see you again. Did you find the boy you was lookin' fer? An hour or two after you left, there was another gen'leman lookin' fer the same boy."

"And what did he look like?" asked Deverell, reaching for his small leather coin bag.

The girl's smile widened. "He were tall and fair with nice manners. Not so generous with the blunt as you were."

"Did you tell him the same thing you told me?"

"Aye." She looked at him from under long lashes,

"Thank you." Deverell laid a coin in her palm and turned away.

"He asked me about you too, sir." Her eyes had a smug look.

Deverell turned back. "About me?"

"He wanted to know if you'd been here askin' about the feller in the picture. He said he were yer friend, and he was trying to catch you."

"Thanks again, miss." He flipped another coin to her, which she deftly caught.

He took Alexi by the shoulder. "Hurry, Lucian was following me. He may have found Nat already."

Alexi's pony followed Deverell's horse, breathing heavily to keep up with the larger animal's long strides.

"Sir, sir, please slow down. This pony cannot trot as fast as your horse, and there are too many people on the streets to keep up this pace," called Alexi.

Deverell pulled his horse over to let her catch up.

"I want to get to the next place I stayed and see if Lucian followed me there."

She arched her eyebrows and pursed her lips. "And does this innkeeper have a toothsome daughter?"

"Ho-ho, do I detect a bit of jealousy?" He reached out to touch her and reassure her, when he noticed several people watching them.

"Never mind about that. Just follow me." He swung his horse around and set her to a fast walk.

"Visiting our establishment again, sir?" the portly owner said. "We're glad to welcome you back."

"I'll require a room and a bath—two towels, please. I want a cot in the room as well. My groom's not feeling well, and I won't have him sleeping in the stable."

The man gave him a peculiar glance. "If you wish, sir. I'll see what I can do."

That set his curiosity up, thought Deverell.

"Take this valise. I have some errands to run. My groom, Alex, will be here soon. Show him to the room, and send the bath then as well."

Deverell went outside to the stable, where he spoke quietly to Alexi. "When you are done with the horses, you may go and ask for Joshua Smythe's room."

"Your room?"

"Of course. A gentleman does not rent an extra room for a groom. You are lucky you are not sleeping in the stable. I've ordered a cot. I'm sure you'll be comfortable."

Alexi turned back to feed the horse and pony, throwing the hay into the crib.

Deverell heard her mumbling under her breath as he walked out of the stable. He grinned broadly. It was just as well he couldn't hear what she was saying.

He looked up and down the street. Where was a likely spot to start his search for Lucian? He strode to the door of the boardinghouse across from the hotel.

An elderly lady dozed at a small desk. He shut the door with a slam, and she woke with a start. She brushed her hand over her eyes.

"Looking for a room, sir?" Her smile revealed several missing teeth.

"I have a question I hope you can answer." He removed his topper.

Her eyes became slits. "Not a Runner, are ye?"

"No, ma'am, a concerned friend. I'm looking for a man, tall, fair-haired. Wears a ring on his pinky and rides a black horse. I believe he might have stayed here about a week ago. Do you remember him?"

"My daughter-in-law runs the place. She maight remember, or one of the maids, they maight. There's the maid now. Ye can ask her."

Deverell repeated the description and saw the glint in the girl's eye.

"A bit of a flirt, would you say?" She gave a little giggle. "He was here four or five days. Stayed to his room except for meals. Then one day when I came to work, he was gone."

So, Lucian had been here while he was across the street and with Nat. "Do you remember what day that was?"

"It musta been a Wednesday, 'cause I only worked Tuesday and Wednesday that week."

"Thank you, miss." Deverell handed her a coin.

"You too, ma'am." He laid another on the old lady's dirty palm.

Lucian had trailed him, knowing he would find Nat. The day he had left disguised as a laborer may have thrown Lucian off the trail for a while. Tomorrow morning he'd leave early and hope Lucian had not found Nat's scent yet.

Chapter Nineteen

Y ou're not going with me. It's too dangerous."

"What will I do while you're gone? I can't stay in this room all day." Alexi stood in front of Deverell, her voice insistent.

"I brought you with me against my better judgment. Where I am going is dirty and unhealthy. The people are desperate and will slit your throat for a farthing. I'll be back sometime this afternoon."

"If it's that dangerous, please be careful, Dev." She reached for him.

"I'll be fine." He held her hand and gaze briefly. "Here's the key to the room. Lock yourself in. I'll be back as soon as possible."

Alexi locked the door and picked up the plate with her breakfast. It was cold and unappetizing. Jam on the biscuit might help.

When she finished, she swept the crumbs into her hand and sprinkled them in front of a narrow crack in the corner of the baseboard. A tiny mouse had poked its nose out of there earlier. Mice had to eat too.

Deverell had brought in the paper for her to read. Thank goodness he didn't hold to that old-fashioned idea women shouldn't read the news for fear they'd see something to upset their sensibilities. Reading soon made her tired, and she plumped up the flat pillow and lay down on the bed. She hadn't slept much last night. Dev had tossed and turned. He was no doubt uncomfortable on that cot. It was disconcerting to have him in the room. She kept wondering what it would be like to have him next to her, to be held close in his arms and warmed by the heat of his body, his kisses on the back of her neck.

She got up and looked at herself in the hazy mirror and saw the flush on her face. She must not think of those things while they were together on the road. That was dangerous. She threw herself down on the bed again and turned on her side.

Sometime later she awoke and felt her stomach growl. She was sure Dev did not mean for her to starve while waiting for him to come back. Pulling on the cap, she tucked all her hair underneath. She shoved her shirt into her breeches and slipped her arms into the rough jacket. With a final glimpse in the mirror, she unlocked the door. She walked toward the stairs and remembered what Dev told her. Running back, she locked the door and dropped the key into her pocket.

She found a table in the back of the dining room and sat on the hard bench. A saucy-looking serving girl came to the table.

"Have ye got the coin to pay fer yer meal?"

Alexi gave the girl an icy stare. "Of course I 'ave. I'm Mr. Smythe's groom. Do you know 'im?"

The girl's eyes widened and went dreamy-like. "Aye, he's the 'andsome one."

Alexi rolled her eyes. "No need to go on like that. I want some stew and a glass of cider."

The girl brought Alexi's meal in good time, hot and savory from the kitchen. The meat was chewy, but there were plenty of turnips and carrots, and it filled the empty space in her stomach. There was no napkin, so she licked her fingers as she popped the last bite into her mouth. She couldn't bear to spend another hour in that room. A visit to Flossie was just the thing.

In the stable she found the hostler taking a nap in a stack of hay by the door. The pony was munching on feed and swishing off flies with her tail. She whinnied softly when Alexi approached.

"Come here, Flossie," she called. The horse ambled over to the gate and let Alexi scratch her forehead. "You're looking fat and sassy."

Subdued laughter and groans came from outside. Alexi's curiosity aroused, she pushed open the back door. Two young stable hands knelt on the ground and watched a bare spot of hard-packed dirt as one threw a pair of dice. He groaned.

The other one laughed. "You owe me another ha'pence, Jack."

"What are you playing?" Alexi asked.

The boy looked startled and grabbed the dice. "Who are ya, and whatcha want to know fer?"

"Name's Alex. Me master's got his 'orse 'ere."

"We're playin' hazard. Wanna join us?"

"I'll jist watch fer a while." She used to play with Lucian and his friends. Pretty good at it too, she remembered. She watched a few more rolls of the dice.

"I'll play with ya."

"Got any coppers? We i'n't doin' this fer nothin'."

"Didn't think ya were. Aye, I've got some farthings and a penny or two."

"Well, join in."

It was a long ride, and, now that he'd warned Nat, Deverell's thoughts were on Alexi. How would she react to the possibility that *her* brother was guilty of murder? He should never have let her come. Tired, he slumped in the saddle and guided his horse into the stable. A bath and a good meal were what he needed.

No one greeted him at the door when he dismounted.

"Here, man, wake up and do your job." He put his boot against the rib of the hostler sleeping in a mound of hay.

"What, who's that? Oh, it's you, sir. Here, I'll take yer horse for ye." The man rose, his joints creaking and stiff. He stretched before he took the reins from Deverell.

A burst of laughter came from the back door, and a familiar voice said, "I won again."

A deeper voice said, "How can you win so often? I'm out of blunt."

"They're your dice. I'm just throwin' them." Alexi's voice again.

Deverell, his mouth set in a hard line, burst through the back door and grabbed his errant groom by the collar. "What have we here? Gambling, I see. Come with me, young man."

"But my winnings, sir."

"Leave them," was the reply.

Alexi could barely keep her feet as Deverell dragged her through the stable. When they were outside, he released her and strode off toward the hotel, muttering to himself.

"Won't listen to a reasonable order . . . puts herself in danger . . ."

She followed at his heels through the lobby and up the stairs.

Deverell tried to open the door of their room, only to find it locked. "Drat."

Alexi took the key out of her pocket and handed it to him. She followed him into the room and shut the door. Deverell sat on the bed and breathed deeply several times. When he looked up, Alexi had removed her cap. With her eyes narrowed and her mouth set, he could see she was seething like a pot ready to boil over.

In a soft voice Deverell said, "Alexi, I asked you to stay in this room."

When she started to speak, he held up his hand. "Hear me out, please. There are things about this world and the people who live in it of which you have no understanding."

She flung her hand out and tried to speak again.

He continued, "If those young men discovered you were a woman, they could easily have ravished you and left you in the alley. Or perhaps a madam could have seen through your disguise and taken you back to her brothel. The values of the people who live in this part of London are not what you've grown up with. You've no idea of the dangers.

"When I heard your voice out there, every scenario I have mentioned and a few others I'll not speak of went through my mind. You can't imagine the cold fear that engulfed me. I know I overreacted and in your eyes I was a brute, but believe me, Alexi, I was much less brutal than most of the men in this place are. I love you, and I couldn't bear it if you were abused."

What had he said? That he loved her. In that moment of anger and fear it had bubbled out of him without a thought.

Alexi's face had turned from crimson to white as he railed on. She went to the cot and lay on it, turning her back to him.

Deverell said no more. He removed his coat and boots and lay down on the bed.

He had not slept well the night before. Sleeping in the same room with Alexi had driven his imagination into a sensual world of delights that kept him tossing and turning far into the early-morning hours. He must apologize again for acting as he had. He'd let his fears overcome his good sense. Good grief, he'd also said he loved her.

He was still mulling over what he'd said when sheer exhaustion overtook him, and he fell asleep.

Alexi lay on the cot, tears squeezing out between her clenched eyelids. She'd stopped shaking, and her heart was beating slower. She couldn't believe he'd pulled her out of there like a naughty child. He'd never acted like that before. She had been safe enough. At least she'd thought she was. The whole thing had humiliated her.

Turning the situation over in her mind, however, she began to see Deverell's point of view. He hadn't wanted her to come with him. She'd persuaded him—tricked him into letting her. He was worried about his brother, and she'd made it harder for him.

But he'd said he loved her. . . . Loved her? She carefully turned over and gazed at him asleep on the bed. His face looked tired, and his hair fell over his forehead like a child's. She tiptoed to the bed and knelt down. Her hands rested on the pillow beside him. She lingered there for several minutes, watching him.

Deverell's brown eyes opened; their golden highlights glinted as he saw her. He reached out and pulled her to him.

Deverell ate with relish. It had been a long time since breakfast. Alexi sat across the table from him.

"When I'm through, we'll be on our way. Knowing Lucian, he'll take a well-traveled road, where he can stay in a decent inn."

"I agree, my brother likes his comfort."

"We'll get the horses and be on our way."

Deverell glanced back at Alexi as she rode behind him on the pony. He thought of how willingly she had come when he had pulled her onto the bed beside him. He had seen trust in her eyes. Trust and love. She had burrowed her face into his chest and trembled. He could still smell the fragrance of lavender in her hair.

"Alexi," he had murmured.

She had looked up at him, a smile lifting the corners of her soft and tempting mouth.

He knew it was a dangerous thing to kiss a beautiful woman as he lay with her on the bed, but he'd pulled her closer, and his lips found a warm invitation. The kiss was tentative and gentle, then deepened.

Then he had pulled back. Alexi's eyes were wide and puzzled, her lips still soft.

He'd released her and rolled off the bed, keeping his back to her.

"Dev?" she'd whispered in puzzlement, her voice low.

"I'm sorry, Alexi. I should not have done that."

"You're disappointed?"

"Hardly. I'm sorely tempted."

A small giggle had escaped her.

He had sat on the edge of the bed and glimpsed her face over his shoulder. It was wreathed in a satisfied smile.

"You imp," he'd said.

Deverell was still grinning from the memory when Alexi rode her pony close beside him.

"A penny for your thoughts," she said.

"They're worth far more than that." He laughed.

The Boar's Head Inn was old, with stone walls and a many-gabled roof. A large stable stood beside it, and a young boy swept the yard with a straw broom. Deverell rode up to the door and called out to the hostler, who was brushing down a beautiful black gelding.

Alexi came up behind Deverell's mount. "That's Lucian's horse, Galahad, the man is grooming."

"Are you sure?" Deverell asked.

Alexi gave a soft whistle, and the horse lifted his head, his ears turned toward the sound. He gave a little snort of recognition as she came nearer.

"It's him. He recognizes me."

She jumped off the pony and rubbed the big black's nose.

"Hey, whatcha think ye're doin'?" said the hostler.

"It's all right," said Deverell. "This horse belongs to a friend of mine." He dismounted and gave the reins to the man. "Take care of the horse and pony. We'll be staying the night."

The man took off his cap and touched his forelock.

"Yes, sir."

The innkeeper was about to give Deverell an argument when he asked for separate accommodations for his groom, but the raised eyebrow was soon lowered by the extra coin Deverell laid on the counter.

He settled Alexi in her room, then entered his own. Deverell threw his coat onto the bed, and the waistcoat soon followed. He washed his hands and face at the basin. A bath would be nice, but he wanted to see Lucian first. His belly knotted with tension. The confrontation with Lucian wouldn't be easy.

A light knock on the door made him turn from the basin with the towel in hand. He opened it to find Alexi standing there with a determined look on her face.

"Alexi? I asked you to wait in your room. You can see Lucian later."

"I'm coming with you. I can help him understand that Nat isn't the murderer."

"I don't want you to come with me. It may be unpleasant."

"All the more reason I should come." Her toe was tapping on the floor, and her jaw was set.

"All right, but it'll be on your head."

The two walked to the room at the end of the hall. Deverell's knock was firm.

The door opened to reveal Lucian in his breeches, shirt, and waistcoat. His eyes widened, and his mouth gaped. "What the . . . Dev . . . Deverell, what brings you here?"

"May we come in, please?"

"'We'?" Lucian looked puzzled.

"I've brought my groom with me." Deverell entered with Alexi behind him. A corner of his mouth lifted at the puzzled look on the other man's face, but his eyes were serious as he spoke. "I've talked to Stanhope, and I know you're looking for Nat. You were trailing me in hopes I'd find him for you."

Lucian flushed. "It seemed like the best thing to do at the time, but you outsmarted me somehow. I still haven't found him."

"Really, Lucian, you can't believe Nat killed someone. You've known him all your life."

"True, but Stanhope made me an offer, and I needed the money. If he's innocent, the police will let him go."

Deverell, angered by Lucian's cavalier attitude, grabbed both his arms and said in a sharp voice, "I have a question for you. Where were you the night Leticia was murdered?"

"Take your hands off me." Lucian's voice was harsh.

The young groom clutched Deverell's arm and spluttered, "How could you?" She pulled off her cap, and her hair fell around her shoulders.

"Alexi? What are you doing here with Deverell?"

"We wanted to stop you before Nat was arrested. I didn't know he was going to accuse you."

Her eyes flashed at Deverell as she pushed him away and stood by her brother.

Deverell didn't look at Alexandra but asked again, "Where were you when Leticia was killed?"

"How dare you ask me such a question? You should know better. We've been friends for years."

"Answer me, Lucian," insisted Deverell.

"How do I know you didn't kill her yourself? I saw you speak to her the night of the party after the fight. You were angry with her, and she laughed at you and walked away."

The color flamed in Deverell's face. He stepped forward as if to grasp Lucian again.

Alexi stepped in between them. "Stop this," she ordered. "I can't believe you are accusing each other."

"He was seen near Leticia's house early the morning of the murder. I have talked to the woman who sold him the roses," Deverell explained.

Lucian collapsed in the chair and put his face into his hands.

Alexandra's face turned pale, and she knelt at his feet and grasped his hand. "No, you couldn't have. Tell me you didn't murder that woman."

"No, I didn't, but I was in the neighborhood. I had gone to see someone else."

"Who?" Alexi and Deverell said together.

Lucian lifted his tortured gaze and looked at Deverell, then Alexi. "Must you humiliate me in front of my sister?"

"Wait for me in your room, Alexi," Deverell said softly.

Chapter Twenty

Alexi started to protest but instead laid her hand on Lucian's cheek and then left the room.

Deverell drew up a chair and turned it around. He sat with his arms crossed on the back.

"Who was the woman?"

"I'll tell you the whole sordid mess." Lucian slumped back in his chair and took a deep breath. "A few months ago I was gambling at Brooks with Helmsley. He said he knew a place we could gamble, a private home. A woman ran the place, and only a select few were allowed in. I went with him. We played cards for a while, and then the lady who operated the place appeared. She was young and devastatingly beautiful. Hair like spun gold, and skin like alabaster. It was Lady Chatham, the widow of the viscount."

Deverell clenched his teeth to keep from speaking.

"You knew her, Dev, before she married Chatham. I remember seeing you with her. You will understand how I was overwhelmed by her. I went to her salons every week for a month. One evening she invited me to stay after everyone left. I spent many nights with her after that. I was in love with her."

"A pity."

"Yes, it was, but how did you know?"

"It doesn't matter."

"The morning Leticia was killed, I went to see Ariadne on a whim. She did not expect me. She had her salons in a rented house, and it was there we had our trysts. I knew she slept there after the gambling parties. I purchased roses that morning, no doubt from the flower seller you spoke to.

"When I arrived, I let myself in with my key and made my way upstairs, when one of the housemaids, who had been lighting the fires, saw me. She grew very flustered and started to say something, but then she fled. I crept down the hall and opened Ariadne's bedroom door. She was not alone in her bed, and I stood there for a moment, stunned. I ran down the stairs and saw the maid in the parlor. I gave her the roses. I am sure she'll remember I was there."

Alexi stood in the middle of the room, her hands clenched at her sides. Maybe Papa was right to keep her from seeing Deverell. How dare Dev have the audacity to accuse her brother, his friend, of murder?

She stalked to the window, where she saw a boy of eight or nine sweeping the courtyard. If she had that broom, she'd sweep Deverell Bromfield right out of her life. But how could she, after that kiss?

A short time later there was a soft knock on her door.

"Who is it?" she called.

"It's Lucian. May I come in?"

She crossed the room, opened the door, and threw herself into her brother's arms. If his legs had not been braced, he would have fallen into the hallway.

He held her. "Everything is all right. Deverell and I understand each other. He's afraid for his brother."

"But you don't understand. I let him . . ."

"You let him what?" Lucian held her at arm's length. "How long were you together on the road?"

"Two days, but—"

Lucian interrupted. "Did he touch you?"

"He kissed me, and I wanted him to. But that doesn't excuse him for believing you killed that woman."

Lucian relaxed his hold, and his lips turned up in the barest smile. "He had evidence I was in the area at the time of the murder. He had to know if I was the one."

Alexi turned away and walked back to the window. The storm clouds stretched across the evening sky reflected the turmoil inside her.

"Is Deverell courting you?" Lucian sat on the side of the bed.

She turned toward him. "Father doesn't want me to see him publicly until Nat is cleared of the murder charges."

"That's a wise decision. Where do our parents think you are now?" He raised an eyebrow at her.

"They think I'm visiting a friend's house. You wouldn't tell them, would you?" Her eyes challenged him.

"Don't be a silly goose. I came to tell you I am going to take you home." Lucian sprawled on the bed, his hands behind his head.

"Where's Deverell?" she asked.

"He left for his home in London. He thought you needed some time to think."

"Is he angry?"

"Would it matter?" He turned on his side toward her.

"Y—yes."

"He's not angry. He told me how you tricked him into bringing you. That wasn't wise, little sister."

"I know that now. Lucian, are you really going home?"

He sat up, an uneasy look in his eyes. "I think it's time for me to go home. I hope they'll have me."

She hugged his neck. "They will. I know they will. But you'll have to take me to my friend's. I should never have lied to Mother and Father, but if I stay with Caroline a few days, it will only be a half lie."

"Alexi, you are hopeless." He chuckled.

The butler ushered a smiling Stanhope into the study. It was a masculine room wainscoted in dark wood, the air filled with the scent of aromatic pipe tobacco and musty books.

"Bromfield, I am glad you are home. I have some news."

"Chess, bring us a pot of tea and a light supper," Deverell said as he motioned Stanhope to one of the chairs in front of the fireplace. "Would you like some port?"

"Not now. Let me tell you what I heard. I went to the police again, and they've found a witness, a costermonger, who saw a man leaving Leticia's the morning she was killed."

"Do they know who the man is?"

"No, but the tradesman says he saw the man after seven in the morning. The innkeeper told them Nat came to the hotel before six. The costermonger described the man as tall and fair, and he rode a black horse."

"Sounds like the description the flower seller gave me," said Deverell. He paced the floor, deep in thought.

"One other thing: the witness thought he saw a flash of red on the man's finger," said Stanhope.

Deverell looked up, hope in his eyes. "The flower seller said the man wore a ring. But that still doesn't tell us who he is." He sat on the edge of the chair, his body leaning forward and hands clasped between his legs. He looked up at Stanhope. "I found Lucian. He's come home to continue his studies."

"His family will be glad. He'd been gambling heavily, you know. I saw him with Helmsley and his ilk more than once," Stanhope said. He stood and faced the fireplace, his hands on the mantel. "I know you don't think I live a proper life, Bromfield."

"It's just that . . ."

"Yes, yes, I know. I have wondered why you continue to be my friend. Never mind. Don't answer that."

Deverell rose, and the two men clasped hands.

"I'll be going. I am taking Mother to the opera tonight."

Stanhope turned, his hand on the glass doorknob. "One more thing about Helmsley. I saw him the night I hired Lucian to find Nat. He said something we thought strange. He said that the night of Leticia's party, Nat declared that if he couldn't have Leticia, no one would. We thought it was a bit melodramatic, even for Nat. There was something else too. Helmsley said how lucky it was for the magistrate that they'd found Nat's monogrammed handkerchief."

"How could he have known about the handkerchief? It wasn't in the papers. Only my family and you knew about it outside of Bow Street. You are sure that is what Helmsley said?" asked Deverell.

"Talk to Lucian. At the time it escaped my notice, but later I wondered about it."

"Things are beginning to come together, but even if we can put the clues into place, we'll still have to convince the police."

Lucian entered Pelhams & Bentons. He wanted to return the brooch he'd purchased earlier for Ariadne.

A gentleman, sitting with his back to the door, spoke to the gray-haired jeweler. "The engraving on the back of this bracelet is to be polished out."

"We'll try, my lord, but it might weaken the integrity of the piece. The engraving is quite deep."

"Do whatever you need to do, only remove it. Do I make myself clear?"

"Yes, my lord."

The man rose and caught a glimpse of Lucian. He touched his hat. "Lucian."

Lucian bowed his head slightly. "My lord."

The gentleman tapped his gold-headed cane on the floor as he strode out.

Lucian shook his head. "Pompous."

"Yes, sir," said the jeweler. "He is that." He held the bracelet in his hand.

"Did you make that piece here? It's exquisite."

"Yes, sir. It is lovely, isn't it?" He laid it out on the velvet-covered table.

Lucian picked it up. He admired the front and turned it over. He hoped he covered his surprise when he read *My Letty.*

Lucian swallowed and said, "Will you be able to polish out the engraving?"

"If we can't, we'll remove the stones and make a new setting," the man said. "Now, how may I help you, sir?"

Chapter Twenty-one

The sound of the spinning mules assailed Lucian's ears when he entered the side door of the factory. He walked down the gas-lit hall to the cubicle of Deverell's clerk, Edgar.

"May I see Mr. Deverell Bromfield, please?" Lucian asked.

"I shall see if he is available, sir. Whom shall I say is visiting?"

"Lucian Moreton."

The clerk looked at him closely through his pince-nez glasses. "Ah, yes, Mr. Moreton."

Edgar knocked and slipped through the door. A moment later Deverell opened it wide to welcome Lucian.

"Just the man I wanted to see," he said. Deverell removed a stack of papers from a chair and offered the seat to his friend.

Lucian placed his hat and cane on the desk.

"I have good news," said Deverell. He took a seat behind his desk. "The police found a witness, a costermonger, who saw a man leaving Leticia's after Nat did."

Lucian sat forward. "Do they have any idea who he is?"

"No, but he corroborates the flower seller's story about a tall man on a black horse. Also, he said he saw a flash of red on the man's hand—a ring, no doubt."

"That doesn't tell us much," said Lucian doubtfully.

"But the police are looking into it, and it gives them another suspect besides Nat."

Lucian's eyes bright, he put both hands on the desk. "I saw Lord Brendan Helmsley today, and you will never guess what he was doing."

144

"I'm sure I couldn't." The lines around Dev's mouth showed disgust.

"He was at the jeweler's having some engraving removed from the back of an expensive sapphire bracelet."

Deverell shrugged. "Why should that be of any interest?"

"It was engraved to *My Letty.*"

"Hemsley!" he shouted. "It's beginning to make sense." Deverell stood and paced behind his desk, his chin cupped between his fingers. "Stanhope told me what he said about Nat's vow to have Leticia. He also knew about the handkerchief," said Deverell.

Lucian continued the list, ticking the points off on his fingers.

"He is fair-haired, tall, and I know he owns a black horse. I do not remember a ring, though. We must find out if he wears one with a red stone. Do you think we have enough to give the magistrate?"

"No. Don't forget that Helmsley's nobility. They're not easy to bring to trial and harder to convict. Come to the house about five this afternoon, and bring Stanhope. We must have a plan, and we don't want to make a mistake. We must know if Helmsley is the murderer."

"I'll go to Stanhope's hotel now. We'll see you at five." Lucian put on his hat and picked up his cane. He paused. "Have you seen Alexi?"

Deverell's face grew serious. "Not yet. How is she?"

Lucian heard the softness in Deverell's voice. "She would be a lot better if she heard from you, you idiot."

Deverell's face flushed. "I was afraid she wouldn't speak to me."

"Then write her, gudgeon." Lucian strode out the door.

Deverell sat with his elbows on the desk, his hands clasped in front of him. Alexi. Would she ever forgive him for questioning her brother about the murder? He had to see her, but first he had to settle this business about Nat. He left his office and walked down the hall to speak to his father.

"I'll be leaving at four today, Father. I'm meeting Lucian and Stanhope at the house."

"You have more news?"

"I think we're making headway, but I can't talk about it yet. Only, if you hear some strange things about my behavior in the next few weeks, please know that I'm doing everything I can for Nat."

"The maid will bring tea soon," Deverell told his two friends. "I've written down the points we talked about earlier, Lucian. I'm sure you've filled Stanhope in."

"Since you know Helmsley, Lucian, why don't you attempt to become a confidant?" asked Stanhope.

"I am afraid Lord Helmsley and I aren't on the best of terms; in fact, we're hardly speaking," said Lucian.

"I'll try to find out about Helmsley, but not from him. There's another source," said Deverell.

Frown lines formed on Lucian's brow. "You can't mean Ariadne?"

"The same. She's close to him."

"They're thick as thieves." Lucian's laugh was brittle. "I don't think Alexandra will take kindly to this idea."

"I don't like it myself, but there's no one else. I've wrestled with it all afternoon."

The butler knocked and entered. The maid followed him with a tray and set it on the desk. She filled three cups with tea.

"Thank you, that will be all, Daisy. Let's eat, gentlemen. I've asked for cold meats and bread, not those little watercress sandwiches the ladies are so fond of. There's something stronger to drink on the sideboard, if you'd like."

The three men stood around the desk filling their plates with roast beef and sliced breast of chicken.

"Speaking of women, Dev, just what are you going to say to Alexi?" Lucian asked as he sat and crossed one leg over the other, the better to balance his plate.

Stanhope made himself at home behind the desk.

Deverell sat by Lucian and set his cup on the side table. "I sent a note over by messenger this afternoon after you left. I will see Alexi later this evening."

When the men had assuaged their appetites, Stanhope asked, "How do you suppose to get into Lady Chatham's good graces, Bromfield? You hardly run with her set."

"We have a previous relationship. I hope to rebuild it enough to find out about Helmsley."

"You're treading on dangerous ground, Dev. She's not a woman to be dealt with lightly," said Lucian.

Dev got up to pour himself another cup of tea. "Oh, but there I disagree with you. That is the *only* way to deal with her. Never trust her, never believe her—take everything she says lightly."

"It is all coming back to me. You were once her steady escort, and something went wrong," said Stanhope.

Deverell leaned against the bookcase, cup in hand. "A title got in the way, for which I'm now very grateful. I only plan to find out if she knew whom Helmsley was seeing on the sly. It would also be helpful to find out if he is in the habit of giving very expensive jewelry to his Cytherians. One of you should be able to tell me where I'm likely to find Lord Helmsley or even Lady Chatham of an evening. I'll have to put myself out in the public eye for a bit. Could you lend me some money, Stanhope? My pockets aren't that deep."

"Whatever you need, my friend, it's a gift. I shall squire you around until you feel comfortable, then I shall leave you to it."

"Lucian, is there anything you can think of that might help me with Hemsley?"

"Play ignorant. He loves to lord it over others with his superior knowledge and rank." Lucian stood and clasped Dev's shoulder. "Be careful. If he is the killer, he might kill again."

"I've come to see Miss Alexandra. Can you tell her I'm here?"

"She's expecting you, Mr. Bromfield. I'll take you to her."

When Deverell entered the room, Mrs. Moreton put down her embroidery and rose from her chair. "Deverell, so good to see you again. I hope your family is well."

"As well as can be expected, Mrs. Moreton," Deverell said as he bowed over her extended hand.

"Have you any news about the boy?" she asked with a concerned look in her eyes.

"We're working on new evidence and hope to know soon."

"I'm glad to hear that. Alexandra, I shall be in my room if you should need me." She left the door open as she retired.

Deverell turned to Alexi. "You look lovely this evening."

"Thank you." The stiffness of her posture softened, and her eyes answered his with a questioning glance. "Lucian told me you were working on a new suspect."

"We are, but it is confidential. Please don't ask for an explanation." He took her hand and led her to the sofa. "I'm sorry that I angered you."

"Lucian explained it. I was glad to receive your letter this afternoon. You stayed away so long." She leaned back against the pillows and looked up at him.

He sat close beside her. He turned her face toward him with his fingertips and kissed her.

"I shall be very busy and will not see you for a while. No matter what you see or hear, I love you and no one else. Will you please remember that?"

"Yes, Deverell." She caressed his jawline, her head resting against his shoulder. "Will you be in danger?"

"I shall be very careful."

He kissed her again. This time his mouth lingered on hers, demanding and eager. When he released her, Alexi's eyes were wide and luminous. He could feel her breath on his face from her partially opened lips. He wanted to kiss her again. Instead he stood and drew her hand to his lips.

Alexi watched him leave. She could not speak a word. What was that sweet, aching sensation that she felt deep inside? Why had no one told her one kiss could make her want more?

Deverell lounged on the sofa in the study, his legs stretched in front of him, his gaze on the fire. He was walking into a spider's web. Silken threads woven by a woman who was adept at catching men for the mere pleasure of destroying them. If only there was another way to clear Nat's name. He'd tried but couldn't think of one. Ariadne was beautiful, clever, and alluring. Would he be entangled before he was aware? No. No, he loved Alexandra. That seductress wouldn't ruin his life twice. He must think only of Nat and Alexi.

Chapter Twenty-two

Stanhope met Deverell at one of the places Helmsley was known to have dinner often.

"Lucian and I visited the jeweler this morning, and he won't remove the engraving or give the bracelet back to Helmsley until we finish our investigation. Of course, that was after I bought an expensive cameo for Mother and promised him more business soon."

Deverell chuckled. "I can always rely on you."

Stanhope tapped Deverell's arm. "There's Helmsley with another gentleman at a table near the wall." Stanhope led him in that direction.

"Hello, Helmsley. Haven't seen you here at the club for a while. How are you?" asked Stanhope.

"Fine. You're looking up to snuff."

"Thank you. You remember Deverell Bromfield."

After a slight hesitation Helmsley replied, "Of course. This is my friend Sir John Matherton."

Sir John rose. "I have to leave now—another appointment, you know. Thanks for having dinner with me, Helmsley. Nice to meet you gentlemen."

"Sit down and join me in a glass of port," Helmsley said. After the two men seated themselves, he asked, "What are the two of you up to this evening?"

"I'm looking for some excitement. Life has been boring of late. Too much time in the office," said Deverell.

"Stanhope, you should be able to help him," said Helmsley.

"I would, but I have a previous engagement, so I'm afraid he's on his own."

The waiter brought the port on a tray. He set a glass in front of each man and the bottle in front of Helmsley, who poured each one a generous portion.

"Here's to an evening of excitement for us all," he said. "I may be able to help you out, Bromfield. What are you looking for—gambling, drinking, women, cock fighting?"

"Some cards or dice might be just the thing," Deverell responded.

"I could introduce you to one of the clubs." He leaned forward in his chair. "Or you might like something more private. A lovely lady is holding a salon this evening. There will be a select few there, but the stakes will be high. Does that interest you?"

"It might. Where is this place?"

"I was going there myself. I would be glad to take you with me. I have my curricle."

"Good. I can tie my horse behind."

"It does not start until later, so we can relax and enjoy our drinks." Helmsley leaned back and stretched his legs under the table.

Stanhope saw Deverell's hand relax around the stem of the glass. "Now that you are engaged for the evening, Bromfield, I shall be on my way. Thanks for the port, Helmsley. Good night."

"Good man, Stanhope," Helmsley said as he watched him walk away.

"One of the best," replied Deverell.

Later Helmsley pulled the curricle in front of a narrow, three-story dwelling in a cul-de-sac. Four streets over from Leticia's home, thought Deverell. The house was light-colored with dark shutters. The windows were heavily draped, but light showed through a narrow opening between them. Three quick knocks on the door brought a footman to let the men in.

"Welcome, Lord Helmsley." The man took their hats, coats, and walking sticks.

A petite woman in a shimmering blue dress that clung to her curves stood with her back to the door. She was talking to two men. One of the men moved closer, and peacock feathers in her hair brushed his cheek. Deverell watched her for a moment. Her figure was fuller than he remembered, but he could see she was even more seductive. Memories flooded his mind. He'd have to keep his wits about him.

There were five small round tables set up for cards and two long tables for dice. Deverell estimated that about twenty men and five women were in the room. Two chandeliers were suspended from the ceiling, and several gas sconces adorned the walls. A haze of cigar smoke hung in the air, and he heard the clink of glasses on the tables. Murmuring voices and the occasional shout of a winner filled the room.

Lord Helmsley introduced Deverell to two gentlemen watching a game of poker. Notes were stacked on the table, and piles of coins lay about. Deverell was amazed at the amount of money the men threw down with such a cavalier attitude.

A hint of jasmine perfume floated around him, and a husky voice called his name.

"Deverell, I had to make sure my eyes did not deceive me. It's really you." Ariadne's smile was warm and her hand on his arm insistent. "Come, we must talk."

She led him to a small room and closed the door.

It was an elegant sitting room, he thought. A small sofa upholstered in gold was drawn in front of the fireplace. Blue damask chairs on either side made an intimate grouping for four. A tall cupboard enclosed with glass doors stood against a wall, and a sideboard held glasses and several decanters. Wax candles in a small gold chandelier and the candelabrum on the sideboard lighted the room. White drapes pulled back by gold tassels against pale blue walls gave the room a cool feeling, like that of its mistress.

"Please, sit down. Would you like a drink?" She gestured toward the decanters on a side table.

"No, thank you." He sat down in one of the blue chairs.

"Keeping your head clear for the gaming tables?" Ariadne chose the sofa. "I was surprised to see you, Deverell. I did not know you liked to gamble."

"I was bored. All work and no play makes Jack a dull boy. I must say, I hadn't expected Lady Chatham to be holding this salon either." Deverell leaned back in the chair and crossed his legs at the ankles.

"When my husband died a year ago, the country property and most of his funds were entailed to his nephew. Chatham was hoping for a son to secure the inheritance, but that was not to be. I am allowed to keep the town home, and there is a monthly stipend until I die if I do not remarry. I needed another income, so here I am. It's all quite enjoyable, not to mention lucrative." She smiled and shrugged her shoulders.

"You always knew what you wanted and how to attain it." He used to think her voice was like silver bells; now it sounded as frosty as ice in winter.

"Not always, Dev."

He could have sworn a shadow of regret crossed her face. She was a fine actress—he'd give her that. "You're Lady Chatham. You have a lovely home and a lucrative business that keeps you surrounded by men, no doubt throwing themselves at your feet. What more could you want?"

She dropped her gaze to hands clasped lightly in her lap and spoke so softly he had to lean forward to hear. "The one man I have always loved."

There was the bait. He reached over to touch her arm, and she raised her gaze to his. He met it with a look that was warm with promise.

"Who would that be, Ariadne?" Deverell asked.

"You know, Dev. It's always been you."

He bit his lower lip to keep from blurting out a renunciation.

She moved closer to him. She would be in his arms in a moment. He leaned back. "You are as beautiful as always. You've not changed at all." He smiled, conveying admiration with his eyes. Well, he admired her acting.

She stood and straightened her skirt. He could hear the swish of the fabric as she walked to the cupboard. A small china figurine lay in her hand when she returned.

Her voice low and sultry, Ariadne said, "Hold out your hand."

In his palm was a miniature spaniel like the one she used to own. He had given her the china piece the Christmas before they became engaged.

"Do you still have Taffy?" he asked.

"Yes, but she is getting quite old and fat now. I don't take her out of the house anymore." She sighed. "Do you remember when you gave me this china dog?"

"I remember."

"I've kept it all these years to remind me of what I lost." There was a tear in her eye ready to spill down her cheek.

Deverell took her hand and kissed her fingers, then turned it over and placed the dog in it.

"I am glad you remembered. I have remembered too," Deverell said.

"You've never married." It was not a question.

"No. There has never been anyone like you." That was the truth.

A soft sigh escaped her inviting lips.

Deverell rose. "It is getting late, and I must leave. Would you like to attend the theater with me on Friday? I hear they are performing Shakespeare's *The Taming of the Shrew*."

She raised her eyebrows and gave him a flirtatious smile. "If I did not know better, I would think you were trying to tell me something."

"I am asking you to the theater, that is all," he replied.

She bowed her head. "I shall be glad to go with you."

She accompanied him to the door and watched him mount his horse. Even more handsome than she remembered, he was a man of passion. That would be a welcome change from the viscount. The Bromfield family business had done well, and someday it would be Deverell's. Maybe he wasn't such a bad catch after all. She'd wait and see.

Chapter Twenty-three

Aren't the roses lovely?" Alexi bent down and pulled a weed from the flower bed.

"Your mother has a real touch for growing them. Oh," she interrupted herself. "You'll never guess, but Mother and I went to a play on Friday night," said Caroline.

"I'm surprised your mother would go to a play. She hardly ever goes out."

"Since she has become friends with Mrs. Murchison, she's been out several times. She's staying at the lady's home for the next few days, so I was free to come visit you."

"What play did you see?"

"*The Taming of the Shrew*. It was well done, especially the female lead." She tucked her arm in Alexi's, and they continued their walk. "Have you seen Deverell lately?"

"It's been almost a week since I last saw him. He said he would be busy for a fortnight."

"Hmm." Caroline bent over and brought a yellow rose to her nose.

"What does that mean?"

"Nothing." The look in her friend's eyes was cautious.

"Caroline, you cannot fool your old friend. What is it you know?" A large lump like cold pudding congealed in her stomach.

"Deverell was at the play."

"Yes?" The lump flew to her throat.

"He was with someone."

Alexi turned and took her friend's arms in a tight grasp. "For goodness sake, just tell me."

155

"Mama said it was the young widow of Viscount Chatham. I'm sorry."

Alexandra bit her lower lip and released her friend. "I'm sure there's some explanation."

"I am sure there is too." She put her arm around Alexi's waist.

When they came indoors, Caroline excused herself and went up to her room. Alexi sought out her mother and found her in the parlor. "Here you are, embroidering again." Alexi walked over to the window, pulled the sheer aside, and gazed out. She turned and rested her hands on the back of the sofa.

Her mother set the pillowcase in her lap. "What is it, dear?"

"Do you know a woman called Lady Chatham? I've heard the name, but I can't remember who she is."

"Do you mean Ariadne Barrington? Her husband was Edward Barrington, the Viscount Chatham. I believe he died over a year ago."

"What do you know of her?"

Isabel hesitated. "She was once a close friend of Deverell's. They were engaged to be married before she met the viscount. Why do you ask?"

"Caroline saw her at the theater the other evening. That's all. Is she very beautiful?"

"I've not seen her in three years, but she was stunning." Her mother's eyes were troubled.

Alexi sighed and left the room. She hurried through the kitchen and out the back into the rose garden. Her skirt caught on a thorn, and she gave it a yank, tearing the garment.

"Darn."

"In a foul temper, I see, my dear sister. What's caused the outburst?"

"Lucian, I didn't know you were back from your ride."

He took her arm and tucked it under his. "Let's walk to the orchard, and you can tell your big brother what is bothering you."

"Lady Chatham."

Lucian swallowed hard. "What about Lady Chatham?" His voice was strained.

She looked up at him. "Do you know her?"

"I've met her once or twice." His eyes didn't meet hers.

"Is she as beautiful as they say?" Her voice quavered.

Lucian cleared his throat. "Beautiful? Yes, she is very attractive."

"Deverell took her to the theater last week."

"You've no need to worry. She's not the kind that men marry."

Alexi stood motionless and in a flat voice said, "Then there is only one reason he was with her."

"No, that is not what I meant. Please, listen to me," cried Lucian, but Alexi fled toward the house.

That evening Alexandra, too restless to sleep, sat with a warm comforter snug around her. Deverell had said he loved her. Could she trust him? He was with the sophisticated Ariadne, the woman he had once wanted to marry. Lucian had said she wasn't the kind men married. Maybe if Alexi was in London, she could do a little investigating of her own. Her friend was going home tomorrow. If she suggested a shopping trip, Caroline would invite her to town.

Deverell came down the stairs dressed in his black evening clothes with a snowy white waistcoat and a square sapphire pinned in his intricately tied cravat.

"You look particularly well this evening. Deverell, I hear you're seeing Ariadne again. Is this true?" His father looked perplexed.

"I'm seeing her tonight."

"But, Deverell . . ."

"Don't worry; it's necessary to help Nat."

"All right, I guess you know what you're doing, but be careful."

He took a firm grip on his father's shoulder. "I shall. Believe me, I shall."

Alexi looked across the table in the London tearoom at her friend. "I'm sorry about your ankle. Do you think you can walk on it now?"

Caroline set it tentatively on the floor and winced. "I've

ruined our shopping trip, and I was looking forward to buying a new bonnet."

"It wasn't your fault. That driver was careless. He came so close, I was afraid you were going to be run over. I'm thankful that it's only your ankle that was injured."

"It was frightening, I must admit. My heart was in my throat when the wheel brushed my skirt. I must have stepped on a pebble when I jumped back. If you hadn't grabbed my arm, I would have fallen."

"Let me pour you a cup of tea. That will put some color back into your cheeks. We'll go home when you're feeling better."

The girls chatted, drinking tea until Alexi could see the pink returning to Caroline's face.

"I'll hail a cab and come back for you." She patted her friend's hand. "We'll shop another day. You must have your bonnet."

Alexandra stepped out the door and bumped into a tall gentleman in a tall hat and caped coat. "I'm sorry, sir. I was looking for a cab."

The gentleman removed his topper and bowed. "Think nothing of it, ma'am." He raised his eyes and smiled. "Miss Moreton. I believe we met at the opera some time ago. May I be of service? You said you were looking for a cab."

"If you'd flag one down for me, I'd be most grateful, Lord Helmsley." She blushed as she thought of what Deverell had said about the man.

"Ah, you do remember me." He smiled. "I'd consider it a great pleasure to take you to your destination in my own coach, which is even now coming down the street."

"That would be most kind of you, sir, but a cab will do very well."

"Alexi?"

She turned to see Caroline in the door of the tearoom. "Oh, dear, you mustn't walk on your ankle."

In an instant Helmsley was beside Caroline. Bowing, he said, "I am a friend of Miss Moreton's. Please allow me to help you." He offered her his arm, and Alexi hurried to her other side. "My coach is right here. I would be glad to take you ladies home."

"Oh, thank you, sir. You are too kind." Caroline looked up at him with a smile of relief.

Alexi could no longer refuse his offer, though going with him was against her better judgment. Caroline put her foot down and gave a slight groan.

"I believe it would be much simpler if you would allow me to lift you into the carriage." Lord Helmsley took her slight smile and pink cheeks as an assent. He placed her against the velvet squabs of the seat as if she were a feather.

He turned and offered Alexi his hand. "Where would you ladies like to go?"

Alexi gave him the address of her father's office.

"Oh, surely we can care for this without a doctor," said Caroline.

"I will feel much better if my father looks at it," replied Alexi.

"Is your father Sir Rowland Moreton? He's my father's doctor," said Helmsley. He rapped his silver-headed cane against the carriage roof and gave the driver the address. When they reached the office, Helmsley insisted on carrying Caroline from the coach. Inside, Alexi knocked on her father's door.

"Alexandra, what a surprise." He rose from his desk and kissed her cheek.

"Father, I have brought Caroline to see you; she seems to have sprained her ankle."

Dr. Moreton stepped into the waiting room. Helmsley had set her in one of the chairs and was standing behind her.

"Lord Helmsley was kind enough to bring us in his coach. This is my father, Dr. Moreton."

The two bowed to each other. Dr. Moreton said, "Good to meet you, Lord Helmsley, and thank you for your kindness to my daughter and her friend."

"It was my pleasure to help the young ladies. Now that they are safely in your hands, I will take my leave."

Alexi smiled at the man. He seemed polite and quite the gentleman. She wondered why Deverell didn't like him.

The next evening Caroline and Alexi huddled together whispering as they waited in the Theatre Royal for the play to begin. "Isn't this exciting? I don't attend the theater often," said Alexi, "and I've never been to one this magnificent."

"I'm glad my foot wasn't badly sprained so we could come with Mrs. Murchison. She is a good friend of my mother and often asks us to accompany her."

"Eighth-row seats. What a wonderful view we have." Alexi took out her opera glasses and began to scan the boxes. "Too bad the royal box is empty tonight." She turned in the seat to look at those behind her.

"You'll have a kink in your neck if you're not careful," Caroline said with a giggle.

A hush came over the crowd as the lights dimmed. Alexi swiveled around to watch the stage as the curtain began to rise. She took her friend's hand and gave it a squeeze. A sigh of delight flowed through the auditorium as the footlights revealed the Duke of Orsini's palace.

At the intermission Caroline said, "I've always loved *Twelfth Night*. It's so sublimely ridiculous."

"I'm parched," said Mrs. Witherspoon. "Let's find some punch."

They began to make their way through the crush of patrons. Alexi was grateful she had worn her favorite green silk. It matched her eyes. Her hair was swept up in back with two curls arranged over her shoulder. She'd laughed when Caroline's maid had put two ostrich feathers into the upsweep, but Caroline had convinced her they made her look more sophisticated. If Deverell was there, she wanted to impress him. She wanted him to be there, but what if he was with Ariadne?

"Alexi, would you mind ordering our punch? Mrs. Murchison saw a friend of ours with her daughter. You had better come too, Caroline," said Mrs. Witherspoon. She took her daughter's arm.

Caroline gave Alexi an apologetic look as she was guided across the floor.

Alexi turned back to the waiter, when she heard a voice behind her. "Miss Moreton, what a charming surprise."

"Lord Helmsley."

He made an elegant bow as she made her curtsy.

"If I had known you were coming to the theater, I would have offered you a ride in my carriage and a seat in my box. Is Miss Witherspoon with you?"

"She and her mother are visiting a friend just around the corner. I have come to get some punch for us."

"You will allow me to do that."

Her face flushed. "That's quite unnecessary, sir."

"It would be my pleasure." He moved to place the order and bumped into a man with his back to him. "I'm sorry, sir." Helmsley said.

Even before the man turned around, Alexi recognized him. When he faced Helmsley, he had a smile on his face, until he recognized him. The smile remained, but she could see Deverell's eyes go dead. "It's you, Helmsley."

"Yes, Bromfield, and I have a friend of yours with me."

He stepped back so Deverell would have a full view of her. She tried to catch her breath. A curtsy was all she could manage. In his eyes she saw dismay and alarm. He reached for her hand and started to say something but closed his mouth with a grimace. His eyes flicked over Helmsley and narrowed with anger. His expression turned cold.

"Who is it, Deverell darling?" Ariadne slipped her arm through his with an air of possession.

He smiled down at her. "Let me introduce you to a friend of my family, Miss Alexandra Moreton. Miss Moreton, this is Lady Chatham."

Ariadne held out her hand, and Alexi took it for a brief moment. Icy blue eyes met glowing green ones. Alexi strove to quell the jealousy that surged through her. The woman was more beautiful than she had dreamed but as cold as ice.

The lights flickered, and it was time to return to their seats.

Deverell took Ariadne's arm and, with an anxious glance at Alexi, walked away.

The heat of anger flushed her face, but there was a sinking feeling in her stomach. She bade Lord Helmsley a brief good night in a choked voice and stepped around the corner to find her friend. Caroline gave her an uneasy look as Alexi took her arm and pulled her into the theater.

"What is the matter?" Caroline asked.

Alexi, unable to hide the strain in her face, spoke in a whisper. "I'll tell you later. Don't ask me any more." She sat through the rest of the performance, her body stiff and stomach knotted, awaiting the final curtain.

Alexi was silent on the ride home and refused to speak until they entered her bedroom.

"What happened? You were shaking, and your cheeks were fiery when you came to get me. Mother wondered why you didn't bring the punch."

"I met Lord Helmsley before I could get it."

"My goodness, what did he say to cause you such dismay?"

"It wasn't him. It was Deverell and that woman."

"And who? Oh, no, not Lady Chatham?"

Alexi sighed and plumped herself onto the bed. "The beautiful, the sophisticated, the frozen Lady Chatham."

Caroline tittered.

"It's not funny. How can you laugh?"

"I'm sorry, but it was the way you said it." She sat on the bed beside her.

"You wouldn't have laughed if you had seen the way she acted, as if Deverell was her prized possession."

"I can see why you were disturbed."

"But that wasn't the worst of it. Deverell looked angry when he saw me. Why was he angry with me? I wasn't there with another . . . oh. He may have thought I was there with Lord Helmsley, and I know how much he dislikes the man."

Caroline took her hand. "That must have been it. Maybe he was jealous?"

"But when Deverell told Lady Ariadne I was a friend of the family, he looked at me with such cold eyes, it chilled me to the bone. Caroline, what am I to do?" She took off her slippers and lay back on the pillows. A tear slipped from her eye.

Chapter Twenty-four

The coachman pulled up to the small house on Chesney Square. Deverell stepped down and told the driver to pick him up at nine thirty. Tonight during dinner he hoped he would learn what Ariadne knew about Helmsley and Leticia.

A footman in blue and gold livery answered his knock and took his coat and hat. He led Deverell to a small sitting room that had been transformed into an intimate dining area. Deverell smiled at the table set with gold-rimmed dishes and crystal goblets that sparkled in the light of the candlesticks. The brass candelabra lit the room with a soft glow. He leaned against the mantel and gazed into the small fire. She was the mistress of intimate settings, Ariadne. Poor Lucian hadn't had a chance.

"I'm glad you've come." Her voice was low and breathless as she moved close to him.

He took her hand and brushed his lips over her fingertips. Her blue eyes sparkled, and her lips parted in an invitation, but Deverell didn't succumb.

A look of disappointment quickly covered, she said, "Come, sit down. Would you like a glass of wine before dinner?"

"Please."

She poured two glasses from the sideboard and brought them to the table. He heard the swish of the white silk as she arranged the skirt so that it lay gracefully around her feet. Her alabaster shoulders and bosom peeked above the form-fitting bodice. The musky fragrance she wore would have enticed any man to succumb to the pleasures that were implied.

A knock on the door announced the footman with a tureen of consommé to start the repast. A white fish baked in a lemon-butter sauce followed. The course of lamb was succulent and served with asparagus.

"The food is excellent"—he reached out for her hand—"and the company delightful."

When the dessert was served, she said, "Shall we sit on the sofa in front of the fire? It will be cozier."

After the dishes were cleared away, Deverell turned to her. "Do you think you could help me with a problem?"

He sat sideways on the sofa, his arm stretched across the back. She reached over to touch his hand.

"If I can, I would be glad to."

"I'm looking for a good jeweler. I need to buy a gift. Who would you recommend?"

She lifted her finger to her chin and appeared to be thinking.

"Maybe some of the gentlemen who come here have mentioned a shop," said Deverell.

"The only one I can think of goes to Pelhams and Bentons. It's on the West Side. You may know it."

"Have you seen any of the pieces made there?" he asked with nonchalance.

"Yes, a bracelet. It was of the highest quality."

"Was the person who purchased it someone of impeccable taste?"

"I would say that would describe Lord Helmsley."

Deverell laughed. "For his latest *incognita,* no doubt."

"He intimated . . . well, I really shouldn't tell you." She chuckled.

Deverell leaned closer, encouraging her to confide in him.

"I guess it doesn't really matter. You're not going to repeat it. She's another man's mistress, but Lord Helmsley sees her on the sly."

"Pompous fool."

She laughed and nodded her head. "He said Miss Browning lived just a few blocks from here. Then he showed me the sapphire bracelet he'd had made for her. It was exquisite. I teased him about it because on the back he had it inscribed to *My Letty*. He mentioned he was going to give it to her on the following Tuesday. She was a very lucky woman to have a man who would buy her a gift like that." She gave Deverell a roguish look.

"Has he ever mentioned her since that night?"

"I don't think he remembered anything he told me. He was so drunk, I had to send him home in a cab with his black horse tied behind." Ariadne caressed the back of Deverell's hand with her fingertips.

He took her hand in his. "You'll never know how much you've helped me. Could you do one more thing for me? Write the jeweler a letter of recommendation? Something to the effect of: 'I am sending you Mr. Deverell Bromfield. I told him about the sapphire bracelet you made for Lord Helmsley that was inscribed to My Letty, a gift for Miss Leticia Browning. He is interested in having something made of that quality. I am sure you will be of service to him.'"

He watched her look become one of pleasure. He could tell she thought it was a gift for her.

"Of course I'll write it for you." She went to the sideboard and opened a drawer. It took only a few moments to dash off what Deverell had asked.

Tucking the paper inside his jacket, he said, "I'll visit them as soon as possible. I'm sure they'll have just what I'm looking for."

The footman knocked discreetly and announced that her guests were arriving for the evening.

They both rose from the sofa. Ariadne laid her hands on his chest and kissed him lightly on the lips. An invitation to stay was in her eyes. He didn't notice, as the lace on her sleeve snagged his tiepin.

Deverell held her hand to his heart and whispered, "Thank you for the dinner and the delightful company." He schooled his face to one of disappointment. "I must leave. I knew you would be busy with your guests tonight, and I made another appointment."

Her lips formed a pretty pout. "I hoped you'd stay tonight. I had a special evening planned." Her breath was feather soft on his cheek.

"I shall stay another time." He removed her arms from around his neck

"Promise?"

Deverell smiled.

He stepped outside and wiped the perspiration from his upper lip. *That was close.* He stepped into his coach and gave the driver the address of the hotel. When the driver brought the carriage to a stop, Dev rushed inside.

"Is Mr. Stanhope in his room?" Deverell asked

"Are you Mr. Bromfield?" The clerk smiled at Deverell's nod. "You may go right up, sir. He's expecting you."

He took the steps two at a time, almost knocking over the white-haired gentleman coming sedately down the stairs. "Sorry, sir," Deverell said as he picked up the man's hat.

"What are these young people coming to?" he heard the old man mutter.

Deverell knocked loudly.

Stanhope answered the door himself. "Quiet, my mother is asleep in the other room."

"Sorry. Here's the piece of evidence that will finish Helmsley." Deverell produced the letter from his jacket and handed it to him.

Stanhope read it quickly and let out a whoop, then clasped his hand to his mouth. "Mustn't wake the old girl."

"Well, what do you think?"

"I think it's enough to get him arrested. Nice piece of work to get her to write you a letter," said Stanhope.

"I was afraid she might not testify if I couldn't prove she'd seen the bracelet and knew who the girl was. Ariadne dated and signed it, so it should stand in court. Helmsley was going to see Leticia on the Tuesday morning she was killed," said Deverell.

"That should put the nail in his coffin. Remember Sir John Matherton, the gentleman we met with Helmsley? I saw Sir

John again this afternoon, and he told me Helmsley arrived at his house late Saturday night after my party and left very early Tuesday morning. Matherton's house is only two hours from London. Helmsley could have arrived at Leticia's just after Nat left," said Stanhope.

"Good work."

"We need to get this and any other information you've come by into the hands of the men at Bow Street Station," said Stanhope. "I can go with you tomorrow morning if you like."

"I'll put together the information I have from the house-keeper and the flower girl and meet you here at eight."

The morning was gray, and a light rain trickled off their umbrellas as they walked to the Bow Street station. They shook the water off and closed the parasols before Stanhope opened the door and ushered Deverell in.

"We have come to see the magistrate, please," Deverell said to the pudgy young constable at the desk.

"Have ye got an appointment, sir?"

"No, but we need to see him concerning a case of murder. We have some information about the killer."

The man's eyes opened wide. "Give me your names, and I'll see if he's in his office."

"I am Deverell Bromfield, and this is Fielding Stanhope. We are here about the Leticia Browning murder."

"I'll go right now, sir." The constable ran up the stairs and was soon back, his face flushed from the exertion. "Magistrate Collinsworth will see you now. Up the stairs and the last door on the left."

The two were smiling when they left the police station. "Now that there is no more doubt of your brother's innocence, what are you going to do?" asked Stanhope.

Deverell waved over a cab. The driver pulled in between a coach and a dray loaded with crates. "I'll send a messenger to let Nat know he is safe and then tell Father. I'm sure he'll take the good news to my mother. I must see the Moretons as well."

They were no sooner seated inside the vehicle when the door to the station opened. Two Bow Street Runners hurried out and entered a cab that took off at a fast clip down the street.

Stanhope and Deverell smiled at each other.

"Won't Lord Helmsley be surprised?" said Stanhope.

"Lord Helmsley, you are here early this evening," said Lady Chatham as she walked down the stairs.

"I have come for some of your fine whiskey and a glimpse of your beautiful face."

"Come into the sitting room, and I shall pour you a glass."

Her fragrance scented the air as she walked past him. He admired the way the silk gown molded the curves of her figure and accentuated the sway of her hips. She offered him a chair and poured him a drink from the sideboard. With a flick of her hand she arranged her skirt as she sat across from him on the sofa.

He picked up a tiepin lying on the table and twirled it in his fingers. The stone set off flashes of blue as the light caught it.

"That's Deverell's. I must remember to give it back to him." She took the pin from him and laid it on the sideboard. "I want to thank you for bringing him here. We have renewed an old acquaintance, and I think it shall be profitable to me in more than one way."

"Don't tell me the man is gambling heavily. I didn't think he was the sort to throw away his blunt."

Her laugh was light. "That is not what I meant. We have been seeing each other. Last night he asked me about a jeweler, and I told him about Pelhams and Bentons on the West Side. I remembered the exquisite bracelet you purchased there."

Small beads of perspiration broke out on forehead. "What bracelet?"

"You remember. The one you bought for the girl named Letty."

The whiskey soured in his stomach. "How did you know about that?"

"You told me one night when you were in your cups drinking my fine liquor."

He leaned forward. "And you recommended them to Deverell Bromfield."

"After I described the bracelet to him, he was eager to know where you got it." Her arm stretched out over the back of the sofa.

Helmsley reached over to set the glass down on the table, his hand trembling so much that he almost upset it.

She reached out and touched his arm. "Brendan, are you all right? You look ill."

"Must be the whiskey on an empty stomach."

"Would you like something to eat or a cup of tea?"

"Did you tell Bromfield the girl's name?" he demanded.

"Well, yes, I did. What difference can that make?"

She could see his face was gray and he was perspiring. "Let me call the doctor." Her voice was solicitous.

"No, I don't need a doctor. Just let me rest a bit." He must think. Would Deverell suspect him?

"Your guests are arriving; I will be fine here."

At the door she turned back. "I shall check on you soon. Let my butler know if you need anything."

A few minutes later Lord Helmsley hurried out the front door.

He lay against the seat of his coach, breathing heavily. Moreton's sister was with Deverell at the opera a month ago. Ariadne said she had renewed her acquaintance with him. Who was shamming it? Deverell was straitlaced. Why would he see two women at the same time? *Not unless Bromfield sought information about him.*

Collinsworth looked up as Captain Grimes entered the room. "Did you speak to the flower seller and the peddler?"

"Yes, sir, and with a little coaxing they went with us to identify Lord 'elmsley when 'e came out of 'is club. We had 'em in separate cabs so that one's opinion wouldn't bear upon the other."

"What did they say?" asked the magistrate.

"It's 'im, all right."

"Good. Do you know where he is now?" He didn't like accusing someone of noble birth. He had to be sure his facts were correct, but once sure, there was no sense in delay.

"They expect 'im 'ome about eight this evening."

"We'll be there. Have someone watch the house the rest of the day."

"Yes, sir."

Collinsworth reminded Captain Grimes and Constable Wilson, "Remember, chaps, we're dealing with the oldest son of the Duke of Whettington. We have to walk a fine line, firm but respectful. I expect you to follow my lead."

The carriage stopped at the front door of the most impressive home on the square. Normally men of law were expected to enter by the servants' entrance, but the magistrate used the front door.

A footman dressed in maroon and gold opened the door and surveyed the three men down the bridge of his nose. A scowl on his face and his posture stiff, he looked ready to refuse them entrance.

Before he could speak, Collinsworth held out his card and said, "We are here to see Lord Brendan Helmsley."

The footman read the card with a dour expression. "I shall see if he is in, sir. You may wait here."

The three men stood awkwardly in the entryway with high ceilings and white marble floors. Two large marble columns stood on either side of the wide staircase where the footman retreated.

Collinsworth heard Captain Grimes whisper to his colleague, "I could put my whole house in this room." He turned to the two men and gave them a stern look.

The footman returned with a message. "His Grace will see you in his study. This way, please." He led them to a hall on the left and into a room with a large dark wood desk and a wall of bookcases. He motioned them to the seats near the fireplace and left the room.

Collinsworth and Grimes stood just inside the door, but

Constable Wilson warmed his hands at the fire. "Nothing like a nice, cheery fire on a gloomy day, sir."

Before the magistrate could answer, a portly gentleman with a shock of white hair entered the room. He was dressed in a superbly cut dark brown wool jacket.

Collinsworth grimaced. Weston's, no doubt, thought Collinsworth, and his own boots smelled of horses and hay.

"Sorry, I have just come in from the stables. I have a mare foaling. You wanted to see my son?" asked the duke.

"Yes, Your Grace, we need to ask him a few questions. I am Magistrate Collinsworth of Bow Street, and these are Captain Grimes and Constable Wilson."

"Gentlemen," the duke acknowledged with a slight nod of the head. "Is there anything I can help you with?" He sat down behind the desk and clasped his hands over his belly.

The man wants to appear relaxed, but the twitching muscle under his eye belies it. "No, sir, I do not believe so. We need to speak to Lord Helmsley."

Chapter Twenty-five

Helmsley ordered his coachman to drive toward the East End. His head resting against the seat, he wiped the perspiration from his face. Soon he banged on the roof of the coach with his cane. The vehicle rolled to a stop, and a footman jumped down to open the door.

"Yes, my Lord."

"I need to see Dr. Rowland Moreton. He has an office near here. Find him."

Alexi took down one of her father's medical books and curled up in a corner of the sofa. A grin spread over her face as she remembered how she used to sneak into his library and read them when she was younger. She still hadn't outgrown her curiosity. This chapter on childhood diseases was absorbing. A good subject to teach to the women in the school at Deverell's factory. Warmth surged through her. She could hardly wait to tell him. That is, if she ever got the chance. The specter of Ariadne rose up to haunt her. She returned to her reading, only to be disturbed by a loud knock on the front door. She heard the footman greet someone. She rose and moved to the open library door.

"I'm Lord Brendan Helmsley, and I want to speak to Miss Moreton immediately. It is urgent."

"Winston, who is it?"

"Lord Brendan Helmsley, miss."

"Lord Helmsley?" She moved to the steps. "I'm sorry my father is not at home. If it's an emergency, I'm sure he'll be back soon."

Lord Helmsley brushed the footman aside and rushed up to her. "It is not your father but you I want to see." He kept his voice low. "I have a message from Deverell Bromfield. He gave me this so you would know the message was from him."

He handed her the tiepin.

"Yes, this is Mr. Bromfield's. How did he come to give you the message?"

"He found his brother near my family's country place. I was hunting there today. He asked me to tell you he needed your help immediately with his brother, who is ill. I am to take you to him. Don't let anyone know. You don't want Bow Street to arrest them both."

The chill of apprehension settled over her. She turned and called, "Abby, bring my cloak. We are going out." She continued down the stairs to her father's office. Helmsley followed close behind.

"I need to get my father's medical bag."

Abby carried the cloak to Alexi. "Don't you think you should wait until your parents come home?"

"Deverell said it was most important you come immediately," whispered Helmsley.

"We have no time to lose."

Brendan took the cloak from the abigail and put it around Alexi's shoulders. "Come, I have my carriage waiting." He took her elbow.

Winston opened the door, and Brendan whisked her through it and into the coach before she could pull on her gloves. Abby hurried to keep up.

When the Moretons returned an hour later, the footman, Winston, greeted them with a worried frown.

"I have a message from Miss Alexandra. A gentleman, Lord Helmsley, came in his coach to take her out." He took their coats and the doctor's hat.

"Where would she be going at this time of night?"

"She didn't say, sir."

"Was she alone?" her father asked, misgivings taking hold.

"Her abigail went with her."

Mrs. Moreton grasped her husband's arm. "I don't like the sound of this."

"Neither do I, dear. Winston, tell Bobby to bring the carriage back around front. I will go to Bromfield's. Maybe he knows something about this." Winston helped him put his coat and hat back on, then rushed out to have the carriage brought around.

"Be careful, dear."

"I will, Mrs. Moreton, I will."

"Mister Deverell, Dr. Moreton would like to see you, sir."

"Bring him in, Chess." *I wonder what he wants at this hour?* Deverell rose from his desk.

"Is Alexandra here?" asked her father.

"No, sir, I haven't seen her this evening."

Dr. Moreton slumped into the chair by the desk. His brows knit together. "Do you know Lord Helmsley?"

Dev couldn't hold back a look of disgust. "We're acquainted."

"Alexandra has gone off with him. I was hoping it was here."

"Alexandra has gone somewhere with that man? Alone?" His stomach clenched.

"With her abigail. His father, the duke, is a patient of mine, but what would that have to do with Alexandra?"

"How long ago did they leave?" Ariadne might know something about Helmsley's hideaways.

"About two hours."

"You must go to the Bow Street police station and ask for Collinsworth. He's the one in charge of this case. Tell him Alexandra has gone with Lord Helmsley. While you're there, I'll see if I can find out where he might have taken her."

"You mean she's been kidnapped? But why Alexandra?"

"I'm not sure, but I'll find out." Something had tipped Helmsley off.

After Dr. Moreton left, Deverell took a brace of pistols from his desk. He tucked one into the waist of his trousers and the other into the pocket of his overcoat. His heart pounded, but his mind was clear. From the hall he called to Chess. "Have Queen Bess brought round."

The lights shone between the curtains in Ariadne's house when Deverell rode up. He dismounted and handed the stable boy the reins.

"Keep the horse out front. I'll only be a few minutes." His coat flying behind him, he dashed to the door.

The footman let him in. "Good evening, Mr. Bromfield."

"Please ask Lady Chatham to meet me in the sitting room. I need to speak to her alone."

"Yes, sir. I'll see if she is available."

The rustle of Ariadne's dress caused Deverell to turn.

She held out her hand to him. "I'm glad to see you. Did you come to pick up your tiepin? I left it on the sideboard." Her gaze searched the top of the dark piece of furniture. She ran her hand over it. "That's funny, it's not here. I'm sure I laid it there after showing it to Brendan."

"Brendan Helmsley was here this evening?"

"Yes, about three hours ago. Come, sit down."

"I can't stay. Where was he going from here?" He tried to keep the impatience out of his voice.

"I've no idea. We were talking, about you, as a matter of fact, and he became ill. I left him on the sofa, and when I returned, he was gone."

"Talking about me. That must have been highly interesting."

She smiled. "I told him you asked me about a jeweler, and I mentioned the bracelet he'd given Letty."

That's why he took Alexi. "I need to find Helmsley tonight. Do you know what properties his father owns?"

"A large home here in London, an estate in the country, and a hunting lodge in Essington. Why do you want to know?"

"I don't have time to explain now. May I have paper and pen? I need to send a note."

"You'll find some in the drawer of the sideboard. I must return to my guests."

She gave Deverell a look that told him she was miffed. He smiled. Thank God he wouldn't have to deal with her anymore.

Deverell wrote a note for Collinsworth telling him of Helmsley's lodge in Essington and his suspicion that he'd taken Alexandra there. At the front door he gave the note to the footman. "I need you to find a man to take this to the Bow Street station," Deverell said.

"Yes, sir."

"He must leave immediately. It's a matter of life and death."

"I shall send someone trustworthy, sir." The footman smiled as Deverell slipped him a gold coin. Deverell left the house and headed toward Essington.

Collinsworth and his men waited at Helmsley's London home until late in the evening.

"My son must be staying out for the night. Why don't you return in the morning?"

They bade the duke good night, and the three of them strolled down the street. Collinsworth said, "Grimes, you stay and watch the house. Wilson, wait with him, and bring me word when Helmsley comes home. I'll send someone to relieve you at six A.M., and I'll come back around nine tomorrow morning."

A hackney came around the corner at a fast clip and halted beside the three. A young constable jumped from it. "Sir, I have two messages fer ye."

Collinsworth scanned the first. "Dr. Moreton thinks his daughter's been kidnapped by Lord Helmsley. Into the hack, men. We have to return to Bow Street."

When they were seated, he looked at the other message from Deverell Bromfield. "Bromfield says Helmsley is headed for his lodge in Essington. Which one of you is good on horseback? It seems we'll be taking a ride tonight. We'll stop and pick up the constable nearest Essington."

Chapter Twenty-six

How far is your lodge, Lord Helmsley?" asked Alexi as she peered out the window into the darkness.

"Two hours or more." He laid his head back against the high seat.

"Did Deverell say what was wrong with Nathaniel?"

"Only that he was ill."

"I wonder why Nat is in the country. He was in London."

He leaned forward, his knees touching hers. "You knew where he was?"

"Deverell did." She put her hand to her mouth. He'd told her not to tell.

"You know hiding a murder suspect is punishable by law."

The anger in his tone frightened her. "It wasn't like that. Nat is his brother. Of course, Deverell would protect him."

Lord Helmsley was silent.

Abby had nodded off, her chin on her chest. Alexi lay back into the corner of the seat to think. She closed her eyes, then gazed from under her lashes at the man sitting across from her. Now that the urgency of the moment had passed, she tried to put her thoughts in order. Deverell did not trust Lord Helmsley, yet he had sent him with a message for her. A shiver ran down her spine, setting off a tingling sensation through her whole body. Something was wrong.

Helmsley ran his tongue over his lips and tasted the saltiness of the sweat. The tightness in his chest made it hard to breathe. He leaned his head back against the velvet squabs. Moreton would seek out Deverell. They wouldn't call the police. Miss Moreton had come with him willingly. He would leave the two women in the gatehouse. No one used it. There was money in the safe in his father's bedroom in the lodge. He'd take it and head for the coast or maybe Scotland. If Bromfield followed him, so much the better; he'd kill him. He reached into the pocket beside the seat and palmed a gun. He eased it under his coat and slid it into the waist of his trousers.

The coach lurched to the left and came to a halt with a thud that buffeted its occupants against the side of the vehicle. Shouts and the whinny of frightened horses reached their ears.

The footman wrenched open the door, and Lord Helmsley cried out as he fell into the man's arms.

"You fool." He spat out a string of oaths.

Alexandra and Abby, crushed against the side of the carriage, clung to each other.

"Are you all right, mistress?" Abby asked.

"Yes, I think so." She tried to sit upright.

Helmsley was too busy berating his coachman to help the women as they struggled out of the vehicle. "What do you mean, we have lost a wheel? I thought you took care of these things. There'll be the devil to pay for this."

"We shall fix it, sir, as soon as we can. The footman will find something for you and the ladies to sit on while you wait." Lord Helmsley pulled out his flask and wandered off into the shrubbery.

Abby muttered about the discomfort and inconvenience of missing a night's sleep.

Alexi jabbed her with an elbow. "Lord Helmsley said that Deverell needs me to help him with his brother."

"Do you believe him?"

"He had a tiepin that belongs to Deverell. In the excitement of the moment I believed Deverell needed me. Now I am not so sure."

"Oh, dear, we should have waited for your parents."

"Well, we didn't, so we will hope he was telling the truth."

An hour later the coach was rolling down the road again.

Alexi noticed that Abby was snoring softly in her corner. At least someone was sleeping. Lord Helmsley sat with one leg crossed over the other, drumming his fingers on his boot. He glanced at her periodically, then looked away, but he didn't say a word.

She heard someone calling her name and opened her eyes with a start. She must have dozed off.

"We'll be there soon; you'd better waken your servant," Helmsley said.

Alexi leaned over and gave Abby's shoulder a slight shake. The woman awoke with a snort.

"We'll be there in a few minutes. Don't forget Father's medical bag."

They were passing through a small village. Alexi saw the steeple of a chapel outlined in the moonlight and several cottages with an occasional candle lighting a window.

A few minutes passed, and she could see the faint outline of a high double gate yawning open. The coachman swung the coach through the gate and brought it to a shuddering stop. The footman opened the door and lowered the steps. Alexi could see a house deep in the shadows.

Helmsley called to the coachman, "Give me two lanterns, and drive the carriage up to the lodge." He took Alexi's hand as she stepped down and spoke in her ear. "This is where I left Deverell and his brother."

"I don't see a light inside," said Alexi. Her suspicions were definitely aroused.

"Of course not. The man's a fugitive." Lord Helmsley handed the lanterns to Alexi and opened the door with a squeal of the hinges.

She noticed a heavy board leaned against the outside but thought nothing of it. Helmsley took one of the lamps while she held up the other to illuminate the room. A musty smell pervaded the air. Two upholstered chairs sat in front of a fireplace that held some cold ashes below the hob grate. An Oriental rug lay between the two chairs with an oblong table on it. A poker rested against the wall of the fireplace.

"I left them in this room. Maybe when they heard the carriage, they hid somewhere in the house."

Helmsley guided them upstairs to an elaborately furnished bedroom. A four-poster bed with heavy side curtains stood against one wall. Satin covers and pillows lay on the bed, matching tables on either side and a bureau against the other wall.

When they couldn't be found, Helmsley said, "I shall go outside and look for them. You wait here."

Alexi ignored the thud outside after Helmsley left.

Abby pulled her close and whispered in her ear, "The man is lying."

"I know, but I don't understand why." Alexi's forehead drew up in a frown.

"Did you see the way that bedroom was furnished? This is no ordinary gatehouse. What shall we do?" asked Abby.

"I'll think of something. Let's wait a few minutes, and maybe we can sneak out. We can make it to the little village we passed through. It's not very far. Someone will help us there."

Abby stood to the side of the window and looked out. "The moon gives a faint light to the ground in front, but I can't see beyond the bushes."

"I'll open the door." Alexi gave it a push, but it didn't budge. She tried again, harder this time. "He's barred the door."

She spied the poker by the fireplace. "When he comes back, you draw his attention, and I will hit him over the head with this."

"Lord have mercy on us," said Abby.

"Amen," her mistress replied. "Shh, I hear something." She held the poker firmly. "Someone is coming up the gravel."

Alexi heard the board being lifted and motioned Abby to stand where she would be seen first. Alexi took her place behind the door as it creaked open. She lifted the poker and stepped forward to bring it down on the man's head, when Abby cried out, "No, miss. It's Mr. Bromfield."

The poker clattered to the floor, and Alexi was grasped in Deverell's strong arms. "Thank goodness, I was afraid Helmsley had lied. Where is Nat?" she asked.

"He's still in London."

"Lord Helmsley said he was here with you and that he was ill."

"That's how he got you to come with him?" Deverell shook his head. "I'm sorry, Alexi."

"It was foolish of me."

"Thank goodness you are safe." He buried his face in her hair. "I was afraid the other night when I saw you with that man, but I couldn't say anything because of Ariadne."

Alexi drew back a little. "She's very beautiful."

"She's an ice queen."

"My thoughts exactly."

"You had no need to give her a second thought. I spent time with her only to gain her confidence. She had information I wanted to prove Helmsley killed Leticia."

Alexi's knees buckled, and he grasped her arms. "Helmsley's a murderer?"

"I've suspected him for a while, but I needed proof. Ariadne gave it to me, though she didn't know it."

"Helmsley may have gone to the lodge. He said he was going to find you."

"Are you able to ride?" She nodded, and he pulled the door open. "See that stand of trees? My horse is tied up in them. Take her; she'll hold you both. Go to the village and find the constable. Send him here."

He leaned down and kissed her. "Be brave, Alexi. I love you." He watched the women until they were hidden among the shadows of the trees. Then the faint sound of horse's hooves came on the chilled breeze of the night air.

Deverell replaced the board on the door and hid in the bushes that grew beside the house.

He prayed the Runners had gotten the message and were on their way. The grating of hooves against gravel alerted Deverell to someone's arrival from the direction of the lodge. It must be Helmsley. His hand in the pocket of the caped coat gripped the pistol. He didn't want to kill the man. He wanted to clear Nat.

The horse sidled up to the gatehouse window, and the man bent over to look in. "Where are those women?" he muttered.

Deverell burst through the shrubs, his pistol pointed at Helmsley.

"Who the—?" shouted Helmsley. "You!" He reached for the gun at his waist.

Deverell grabbed for the reins and brushed against the horse's shoulder. The alarmed animal snorted and reared. The reins jerked from Deverell's grasp and threw him off balance. His gun went off, grazing Helmsley's arm. The man brought his horse around and turned to Deverell, firing at him. Deverell dropped to the ground. Blood covered his jacket.

"If he's not dead, he soon will be." Helmsley turned back toward the lodge to get his arm tended to.

The caretaker met him at the door of the lodge and stepped outside. "My lord, some men have arrived, and they are looking for you. They wouldn't say who they were, but one of them is the local constable."

"Tell the coachman and footman to take the carriage away from here by the back road and go back to London. If you or your wife is asked, tell them I have just arrived. Do you understand?"

"Yes, my lord."

Chapter Twenty-seven

The study door burst open. Collinsworth jumped up and alerted his men to be ready.

A tall young man with a florid complexion strode inside. "I understand that someone is here to speak to me. What is this all about?"

"I'm Magistrate Collinsworth, and this is Captain Grimes. We're from London." The high-handed manner of the young noble grated on him, but he kept his voice calm. "This is the local constable, Thomas. We're looking for a young woman, Alexandra Moreton, and her abigail. We have reason to believe they left London with you in your coach."

"I have just arrived on horseback. My coach isn't here."

"Check the stables, Grimes." He made an impatient gesture toward the door, and the captain left at a brisk pace.

"You were seen at the Moreton home this evening and entered your coach with Miss Moreton some minutes later. Correct?"

"Yes, I took her to her friend's house and left her and the maid there."

"I'll need the name and address of the friend."

"I don't remember the name. It wasn't my friend, and my coachman in London will know the address." Helmsley removed his gloves as he spoke.

"I see. We would like to search the lodge and the stables." Collinsworth spoke through gritted teeth.

"What for? I've already told you she's not here." The man's face flushed, and his eyes narrowed.

Grimes came in and conveyed his message with a shake of his head.

Collinsworth knew it was risky to overstep the boundaries with a noble's son, but he had to know if the girl was there. "Grimes, search the place."

Lord Helmsley raised his arm as if to bar the way. He groaned in pain.

"What's wrong?" Collinsworth asked

"I fell and injured my arm on the ride here. I need to have it tended to." Helmsley pulled the bell cord.

Collinsworth saw a red stain and a tear on the sleeve of the man's jacket as he helped remove it. A trickle of blood had flowed down to Helmsley's little finger and onto a gold ring set with a ruby.

The caretaker's wife entered. "Yes, my lord."

"I have injured myself. It needs to be cleaned and bandaged." He sat down in one of the chairs, looking pale.

"Right away, my lord." The woman returned and poured a little wine on the wound to disinfect it.

Collinsworth moved behind the chair and peered at the arm before she smeared it with ointment. "Just a moment. That wound isn't from a fall. It looks like a bullet wound. How did it happen?"

"I told you, I fell from my horse. My gun was in my coat pocket. It went off and injured me." Helmsley stared at the man. "Wrap the arm, woman." When she finished, he eased the shirt over his shoulder, leaned back, and closed his eyes.

Collinsworth was about to speak, when Grimes called him into the hall. "Didn't find anything. There's nothing in the 'ouse or stable that suggest she's been 'ere."

He grimaced "I shall take a different line of questioning with the man. We seem to be getting nowhere."

The two men turned when the front door flew open and the Duke of Whettington rushed in, his face red and his breath short. "Looks like you were a step ahead of me," the duke said.

"It would seem so, Your Grace," replied Collinsworth.

The caretaker took the duke's caped coat and topper. "Your son is here, Your Grace."

Collinsworth and the constable followed the duke into the room where Brendan still sat at the fireplace.

The young man poured himself a drink. "Hello, Father. What brings you here?"

"I was looking for you."

"I assume you have met these, uh, gentlemen." He gestured with his glass.

"Yes, last night. Now, what it is it you wanted to talk to my son about?" The duke took a seat near Helmsley.

"They have been questioning me about a young woman I saw last night. They think I have hidden her away somewhere." He laughed and took a seat.

The duke looked away, but not before Collinsworth saw the frown on his face.

"I must ask you some questions about another woman, Lord Helmsley. It has to do with an investigation we are making into a murder that took place several weeks ago, a Miss Leticia Browning."

Helmsley's face took on a gray hue. "Why should you think that I had anything to do with her murder?"

"We are only here to ask you some questions, Lord Helmsley. Did you know Leticia Browning?"

"She was the mistress of a friend of mine."

"Fielding Stanhope. Have you ever been to her home in Newbury Court?"

"Of course not." His voice was indignant.

"Have you ever given the lady a gift?"

"This is outrageous." Helmsley jumped to his feet, his face mottled. He held his wounded arm with his other hand.

"Where were you on Tuesday morning, May 3?"

The duke was on his feet. "Sir, unless you have some evidence to prove your disgusting accusations, I am going to ask you to leave my house."

"I have evidence, Your Grace, a great deal of it. Here is a receipt for a sapphire bracelet purchased by Sir Brendan Helmsley on April 29. It is engraved to My Letty. I have an affidavit from Lady Chatham that he told her it was a gift for Leticia Browning when he showed it to her a few days before the girl was killed. I have information as to his whereabouts on the morning she was killed. There is more, Your Grace."

The old man sat back in the chair and placed his head in his hands. "It's enough, it's enough."

"You can't believe these people." The young man gripped his father's shoulder. "How can you believe these commoners over me?" His voice was disdainful and his mouth twisted by anger. "I have killed no one. You cannot prove it."

"This time you will have to face it yourself. I cannot help you against this charge." The duke's face was pale, but his voice held authority.

"I am arresting you in the name of the king," said Collinsworth.

Helmsley's bravado and pomposity were gone. He slid down to the hearth. Wilson stood beside him. The only sound in the room was the crackling of the fire and the ticking of the mantel clock.

Collinsworth glanced at the duke slumped over in his chair. *There's a man who believes his son is guilty. The fight's gone out of him.*

The caretaker came into the room holding up an injured man whose coat was covered with blood and dirt. "Your Grace, this gentleman came to the door, and when I opened it, he fell into my arms."

The duke looked bewildered, and Collinsworth took charge. "Lay him on the chaise in the corner." He turned to the local constable. "Is there a surgeon in the village? This man looks seriously injured."

"I'll get him." The constable ran to the door.

Grimes helped the caretaker carry the man to the chaise. "I've seen this man before."

"It's Bromfield," said Collinsworth as he pulled the coat away from the wound. "Looks like he took a bullet in the shoulder. His eyes are opening. Bromfield, can you hear me?"

A groan escaped Deverell's lips. "Helmsley?" He raised up on one elbow.

"It's Collinsworth. What happened to you?"

"Helmsley shot me. I found Miss Moreton and her abigail. They're safe. I sent them to the village. Where's Helmsley?"

"We've arrested him."

"Did he confess to Leticia's murder?"

"Doesn't matter, we have plenty of evidence."

Chapter Twenty-eight

Wwhat was taking so long? Deverell waited in the sitting room of the Moretons' town home, tapping his fingers on the arm of the chair. He hadn't seen Alexi since he brought her home from Essington several days ago. Had she recovered from that ghastly night? His shoulder still ached. The door opened, and Dr. Moreton stepped into the room. Deverell stood and waited for the man to speak.

"I heard you were in the house, and I thought you must have news of what happened. The paper said the police have arrested Lord Helmsley." He motioned Deverell back into his seat.

"Yes, sir, the killer's been caught and my brother cleared of all suspicion. I came to see how Miss Alexandra is."

"She has recovered quite well from her ordeal. Thank you for helping her escape that madman. Ah, here is Emmy with the tea tray. Leave it on the table. Mrs. Moreton and Alexandra will be down in a minute."

Alexandra rushed into the room, then stopped when she saw her father. "Papa, I thought you were with patients." She turned to Deverell. "Mr. Bromfield, how is your injury?"

Deverell stood and, taking her hand, kissed it, then looked into her sea-green eyes. "It's only a slight flesh wound. I have to wear this sling, but it's healing quickly." A look of relief flooded her face, and his lips curved in a smile.

"Well, Deverell, tell us what happened," Dr. Moreton prompted as his wife entered the room and sat beside him.

"Please do," she encouraged. "Alexandra said you didn't talk much in the coach that night."

Deverell sat close to Alexi and told about the harrowing evening. When he spoke of the capture of Helmsley, he took her hand.

"I've heard Lucian mention Brendan Helmsley's name. I don't think he liked him much," said Dr. Moreton.

"I should hope not. He's a murderer," said Mrs. Moreton. "You say Lucian helped you, Deverell."

"He, Stanhope, and I were able to put several clues together and take them to the police. I will be going to get my brother, Nat, tomorrow. My parents are eager to have him home."

Dr. Moreton stood. "I must go. I have patients to attend." Deverell stood, and the man grasped his good shoulder. "I am glad everything has worked out well."

Mrs. Moreton took her leave moments later, and Deverell and Alexi were alone. Deverell took her hand and pulled her up from the sofa. Lavender filled his senses when he laid his cheek on her hair. Her arms around his waist held him closely, and her head lay against his chest. He knew she must hear the thudding of his heart, for he could feel it beating in his throat.

"My dear Alexi," he murmured.

She raised her face to his, and he kissed both of her eyes and then the spray of freckles on her nose. His lips sought hers, hungrily demanding more and more until she drew back.

"Let me catch my breath," she said. Her cheeks were flushed and her breathing ragged.

"I have missed you so, my love," he said before he captured her mouth again.

Nat stood on the dock outside the warehouse, gazing at the night. There had been a drizzly rain for the last two days, but now the sky was clearing. He could see the clouds parting and the moon shining through.

He looked again at the paper in his hand. The police had the murderer, Lord Brendan Helmsley. He was free to go home at last. Deverell was coming to get him tomorrow, and he would see his parents by nightfall. He read the note again. He'd miss Mr. Mullins. He had enjoyed working here. Most of all he would miss Henry. The boy was like a little brother to him. *Don't get all sentimental.* That's what Henry would say.

"Ye're sure in some kind of funk. I been standin' here two minutes, and ya didn't even notice me." Henry stood at the top of the stairs.

"Henry, I haven't talked to you in a long time. I thought you might be angry with me, although I couldn't think of why you would be."

"Nah, I'm not mad, jest been busy."

"I'm glad you came by tonight." He waved a paper in the air. "I have some good news. I'm going home. My brother comes to get me tomorrow."

"Tomorrow?" the boy squeaked.

"It seems like an age since I left home. It'll be great to see my mother and father."

"I'm . . . I'm glad fer ya."

"I want you to know I consider you my friend, and I will come and see you. I promise."

"Oh, sure, that'll be nice. Ya in all yer finery, riding up on a fancy stepper. Ya do have one, don't ya?"

"I have a filly. She's a beauty."

"Goin' home sounds real good. Do you live here in Lun'on or in the country?"

"We have a home in London and a home in the country. I like the country best."

"Yeah, I can understand that. Looks like I didn't know ya very well after all."

"You deserve an explanation, and I've already told Mr. Mullins. You see, there was a terrible misunderstanding, and the police thought I had murdered a young woman."

"Ya a murderer? Were they tetched in the head?"

"I was within an inch of being captured by them, so I ran, and that is how I ended up here, cleaned out of money and needing a job. You saved my life, Henry. I will never forget it."

Nat could swear the boy was blushing.

"It weren't nothin'. You saved my life a few days later."

"I've been meaning to talk to you about that. I followed you home that day and saw where you live."

The boy's eyes widened. "Ya i'n't gonna tell no one, are ye? I don't want to end up in one o' those homes for orphinks."

"No, I won't tell anyone, but please be careful." Nat reached over and put his arm around the boy and hugged him. "I don't want anything to happen to you, my friend."

Henry wiped his nose with his sleeve. "I'll be fine. I have been all these years. I gotta go now. I'll come by in the mornin'."

"Good night, Henry."

"Night."

Nat could have sworn he heard a sniffle. It had to be tough being on your own that young. He wished he could do something to help Henry and the other waifs working on the streets.

Henry hurried down the alley toward the warehouse where he lived. Tears streaming down his face, he stepped on a cat that was skulking through the garbage in the street. The animal yowled and hissed, but Henry hardly noticed. He entered the warehouse and scurried into his little place inside. Throwing himself onto his pallet, he cried himself to sleep.

Mr. Mullins was standing behind the counter when the door to his shop opened and a tall, well-dressed young man with a valise in his hand strode in.

"May I speak to Nathaniel Bromfield, please?" the man asked.

"Ye must be his brother, Deverell. Ye look a lot different than when ye were last here to see Nathan, uh, Nat," Mr. Mullins said.

Deverell chuckled softly and grasped the hand the older man held out. "Thank you for being a friend to my brother."

"He was a good help to me. I'll be sorry to lose him. He's in his room. Ye can go on back."

Nat opened his door when he heard voices and rushed to give his brother a bear hug.

"Hold on a minute. You've knocked the breath out of me," Deverell gasped, and he reached out to squeeze Nat's arm. "You've grown some muscles."

"They're from lifting all the heavy boxes in the warehouse for the last few weeks. I think I've grown up in other ways too," Nat said, his face solemn. "Your arm. You've been hurt."

"Just a scratch." Deverell punched his brother's shoulder. "We need to leave if we want to be home by nightfall."

"I was hoping to say good-bye to Henry again, but he must have been held up. I need to tell Mr. Mullins something. I'll be right back."

"I brought your clothes."

Nat's face lit up. "My own clothes and boots."

Nat went into the store and found the old man moving merchandise to the counter.

"Mr. Mullins, I'm concerned about Henry. He's a clever fellow, and I think he'd be a help to you, if you could see your way clear to hiring him. Someone could come in and put the large boxes on the shelves in the warehouse under Henry's supervision. He'd learn how to do a lot of other things around here too. He reads and writes, you know."

"I do like the boy, and I agree he'd be an asset to me. Joe works next door. Maybe he'd have a few hours during the week to lift the heavy loads. My wife always said she wanted to fatten Henry up. I'll talk to them both as soon as I see them. Thanks, Nathan . . . Nat." He took the young man's hand and patted his shoulder. "Ye come back and visit anytime ye get hungry for a good meat pie."

"I will, Mr. Mullins, and tell Henry good-bye for me. I can't understand why he hasn't come by."

Nat's face lit up when he saw his filly waiting outside the door. She nuzzled his neck and his pocket looking for a treat. He patted her nose and ran his hands down her chest.

"I didn't think I would see you again, old girl. Let's go home."

The two men mounted and turned down the road for the journey home.

Hidden between the walls of the two shops was a lonely little figure. One large tear coursing down his cheek, Henry said softly, "Good-bye Nathan. Good-bye, friend. I'll miss you more than you'll know."

He wiped his face with his sleeve and watched until the men were out of sight.

Chapter Twenty-nine

Mrs. Bromfield couldn't stop smiling. Her boy was coming home. The kitchen was filled with the tantalizing aromas of all his favorite dishes, some of which she had made herself. The sound of voices reached her ears, and she hurried into the hall at the front of the house.

"Nat, oh, Nat, you're home." She embraced him, and he lifted her off the ground.

She smiled, though her eyes were brimming with tears. "Are you all right?"

"I'm fine, Mother, just fine." He bent down and kissed her cheek.

Mr. Bromfield entered the hall. "Good to have you back, son." His voice was rough with emotion.

The two hugged, and Nat said, "I'm glad to be home, Father, very glad."

Deverell leaned against the door frame. "We're famished, and I'm sure you've prepared a feast, Mother."

"I have. Thank you for all you did, son." She put her arm around his trim waist and squeezed him as she looked at him with pride. "How is your arm?"

"A twinge here and there."

"Go and rest. Dinner will be ready in an hour."

The family gathered in the parlor after dinner. A warm and cozy fire crackled on the hearth. Mrs. Bromfield sat on the sofa beside Nat, and Mr. Bromfield, a broad smile on his face, stood by the fireplace. Deverell rested in his chair.

Anne Louise asked, "Have you set the date for your wedding yet, Deverell?"

"I hope to do that tomorrow when I see Alexandra. I would like it to be soon, but I understand women need time to prepare."

"How would you feel about sharing the house in town with me until you find a home?" asked his father. "You would have it to yourselves on the weekends."

"That's very generous, sir. I'll talk to Alexi about it."

"Nat, you're very quiet," said his mother.

"I thought about a new direction for my life while I was away. I'd like to do something for the poor children of London. A young lad named Henry took me to chapel with him several times. That was when I made my decision. I talked to Pastor Belden, and I'd like to start a home for the orphaned children who live on the streets. It's a hard and dangerous life out there."

Mr. Bromfield gazed at his younger son. "This comes as something of a surprise, but if that is what you want, then I say, I'm all for it. I'd like to talk more about it with you tomorrow."

"Thank you, Father. What about you, Dev?" He turned to his brother and saw the smile on his face.

"You never cease to amaze me, little brother, only this time I'm pleased."

Cheerful laughter filled the room.

"Three months?" Deverell and Alexi sat on the upholstered seat in the bow window.

"That's the least amount of time we need to prepare for a wedding. The banns must be read, and then there are invitations, the wedding dress and attendants' dresses, my trousseau, the wedding dinner, the service, the flowers."

"Enough, enough. I am overwhelmed. I concede three months, but not a moment longer." He kissed the end of her nose.

"You missed," she said, smiling at him.

"Missed what?" he asked.

"This," she said. And she kissed him, her lips soft and pliable against his.

He held her for a moment longer. "Are you sure you don't mind living in the terrace house with Father?"

"I think it's wise to wait before we look for a home, and I shall get to know your father better. It will be fine. Oh, Dev, I love you. I don't care where I live," she said as she nestled her head against his broad chest.

The time passed slowly for Deverell but flew by for Alexi and her mother. The Moreton house was a flurry of sewing, shopping, and cooking. Finally the day arrived.

Her attendants sat on the bed as Abby lowered the dress over Alexi's head. "Oh, miss, it was worth every moment it took to sew those bugle beads on. They look like diamonds sprinkled over the skirt and bodice. And the Brussels lace at the waist is perfect."

"These are the earrings Deverell gave me," said the bride.

Abby helped her affix the lovely pearl drops to her ears. Isabel Moreton arranged the veil over Alexi's head and shoulders. Caroline spread the train out.

"The same lace around your waist and the train gives the finishing touch." Isabel handed her daughter a delicate lace hanky. "I carried this when your father and I married. I want you to have it."

"Thank you, Mother, it's lovely." She reached out and hugged her mother. Alexi wiped a tear from the corner of her mother's eye. "Don't cry, or I shall start."

"I have a sixpence for your shoe." Chloe knelt down to slide it into the white slipper.

"And I've made you a garter." Caroline giggled.

"And I am the happiest woman in the world." Alexi's face glowed.

Chloe, Penelope, and Caroline, dressed in lavender silk gowns with floral wreaths on their heads, proceeded down the aisle of the small chapel. The groomsmen, Stanhope, Lucian, and

Nat, dressed in black jackets and lavender waistcoats, stood solemnly by Deverell's side.

Mrs. Eddington played the opening notes of the bridal procession. Alexi stepped slowly into the aisle on the arm of her father, who looked a bit teary-eyed. At the sight of his bride, Deverell could hardly catch his breath. Her dress sparkled and shimmered but no more than the green eyes that held his gaze. A wide band of delicate lace surrounded her tiny waist, a waist so small he could almost put his hands around it. A jolt of love and desire raced through him. The irrepressible child who had once been his shadow had grown to be the irresistible woman who was soon to be his wife. Her father presented her. Deverell took her arm, and his gazed fastened to hers before they turned to face the preacher.

Anne Louise Bromfield inhaled the fragrance of the bouquets of roses, stock, and fern upon the altar and attached to each pew. A beautiful day, she thought as the sunlight filtered through the windows. The piano was silent as the preacher began the ceremony. She exchanged watery smiles with Isabel across the aisle. Deverell and Alexi would suit each other very well.